THE EYES WERE COLD.
THE FACE WAS HARD
AS STONE.

"I gave you fair warning," Cobb told me flatly. "I said there was a lot of mud out here in the swamps to lose you under if you got in my hair. But you didn't get me. You kept right on poking around and shooting your mouth off."

His eyes went the length of me, down, then up—taking their time. His mouth became thin.

"So now it's good-bye, Rome. . . ."

MY KIND OF GAME

Marvin Albert

FAWCETT GOLD MEDAL · NEW YORK

A Fawcett Gold Medal Book
Published by Ballantine Books
Copyright © 1962 by Anthony Rome

ISBN 0-449-13388-5

This edition published by arrangement with Dell Publishing Co., Inc.

Manufactured in the United States of America

First Ballantine Books Edition: July 1989

Chapter 1

THE ROOM SMELLED OF BLOOD. THERE WAS A DRYING CRUST of it along one corner of Lou Kovać's gasping mouth, half a bottle of it hanging over his bed, and more of it dripping through the transparent plastic tube running from the bottle to the needle stuck in the vein of his left arm. The arm was still muscular, but its hairs were gray, almost white. With a sense of shock it came to me that I'd known Lou for so long that I hadn't been aware of his growing old.

The beating had abruptly completed his aging process, as effectively as a wrecking crew ripping out the interior supports of a condemned building.

It was an old man who lay on the bed, fighting for what was left of his life. He panted for each breath. The tortured heaving of his chest under the sheet was weak and uncertain. He fought for his life unknowingly, drugged into oblivion by injections of morphine which had separated his conscious mind from his agony.

The nurse was glaring at me from across the bed and pressing hard at the call button. I ignored her, moving to the edge of the bed.

Whoever had administered the beating had concentrated on him from the shoulders down. His face was unmarked. But it was a cruel caricature of the face I'd known. Where its bone structure had been prominent it now stood out in stark ridges; where the flesh had been taut, it was shrunken.

1

The skin of his bald head and gaunted face was splotchy gray, his lips like dirty wax. His closed eyelids lay flat, as though his eyes had retreated deep into their sockets to escape what had been done to him.

Whatever they'd beaten him with—baseball bats was the best guess—had been used with systematic savagery.

They'd smashed both his kneecaps and his right hip, shattered his rib cage. His broken hands lay on either side of him on the sheet, held in complicated structures of wired splints.

The damage done to his stomach, kidneys and other organs was so severe that it had taken two surgeons over an hour to stop his internal bleeding, before they could begin work on his shattered bones.

I was staring down at him frozenly when a doctor bustled into the surgery recovery room.

"What are you doing here?" he snapped at me. "No one other than hospital staff is allowed in this room."

The nurse on the other side of Lou's bed said quickly, "I told him that, doctor."

"She told me," I acknowledged, not looking up.

"Then what are you doing in here?" he demanded.

"I'm his friend," I said tonelessly. "I came to see for myself."

"I don't care who you are, you have no business being in this room. He's in no condition . . ."

"What *is* his condition?" I raised my head and turned it and looked at the doctor. "Will he live?"

He met my eyes and some of the indignation leaked out of him. "Yes—he'll live. That is . . ." The doctor tore his eyes from mine and looked at the man on the bed. "He's going to live. But at this moment, and considering his age, I can't say what he'll be like for the rest of his life. After what Mr. Kovac has been through, you see . . ."

"I do see," I told him. "Thank you." I walked past him and went through the door.

Outside in the corridor I leaned the backs of my shoulders

against the wall and fumbled a Lucky from my pocket. I got it lit and sucked my lungs full of smoke. After a time I let the smoke out, slow. When the cigarette was down to a stub, I crushed it under my heel and went to see Art Santini at Homicide.

Lieutenant Santini was behind the desk in his small gray office at headquarters when I entered, filling out a case report with a red ballpoint pen. He was a plump man with a round, deceptively bland face. As I closed his door he raised his head and stuck the end of the pen between his even white teeth, leaning back in his chair. His dark liquid eyes watched me lower myself into the other chair, between the filing cabinets and his desk. We looked at each other.

Santini put the pen down on the unfinished report. "They let you see him, Rome?"

"I saw him." I got out a cigarette and rolled it between my fingers. Then I broke it in half and threw it into his wastebasket. "You'll be yanked off the case," I told him. "Lou's going to live. So it's not murder, or even manslaughter."

"There's still attempted murder," Santini pointed out.

"Not even that. Assault and battery. They didn't intend to kill him. They did what they set out to do. Not more. Not less. They knew how. Professional goons."

Santini nodded. "Uh-huh. How come? What was he doing that'd get him that kind of attention?"

"I don't know," I said. "I hoped you could tell me."

"Well, I can't. We went over his office and apartment real careful. There wasn't a thing to tell us what he'd been working on lately. I guess we'll have to wait and find out what gives from Kovac himself, when he comes around enough."

"Don't count on that," I said softly. "It'll be a helluva long time before Lou's in any shape to talk. Even then, he may not remember anything. A working-over like he got doesn't usually leave a man much to go on with. Even money he'll be doing the rest of his living in a nursing home.''

I stared bitterly at the dusk shimmering in the fat shaft of Florida sunlight that lanced through the single window of Santini's office. "He's an old man, did you know that? Too old to be playing tag with hoods.''

"Yeah,'' Santini said. "He's been around a long time. Used to be on the force back in the old days, before he shifted to private detective work.''

I nodded. "He was my father's best friend. They started as rookies together. When I was born, Lou was made my godfather. When I quit the department, he helped me get my private detective license.''

"I know,'' Santini said. "That's why I called you. Kovac hasn't got any close kin around, has he?''

"Nobody.'' I stared back into the hot sunlight streaming through the window. Then I looked at Santini. "All right. What *have* you got on it so far? Anything?''

Santini sighed. "Damn little. Some woman who wouldn't identify herself phoned in and said she'd heard what sounded like somebody getting beaten up in the alley next to the building where Kovac has his office. By the time a prowl car got there, Kovac was all by himself in the alley. The guys who'd done the wrecking job on him were gone. We haven't turned up anybody so far who saw them.''

"And that's it? Nothing more?''

"There's one thing.'' Santini hesitated. "It may not mean anything, though.''

"Tell me.''

"We found a motel receipt in Kovac's wallet. He was paid up for a full week in advance. The week still has three days to go. A place called the Seaview Motel—in Coffin City.''

I knew of Coffin City, an ironic name for a city. Its founder had been John Coffin but lately the name had a less pleasant identification. It had a number of reputations. Most long-standing was its reputation as a distribution center for moonshine turned out by illegal stills hidden away in the Everglades and Big Cypress Swamp. Since the war Coffin City had also acquired a reputation as an anything-goes tourist trap. Still more recently, it had been experiencing a building boom in home developments for retired couples.

"Of course," Santini said, "it may not mean he was working on a case. Maybe he just went there for a vacation."

"Coffin City's not the kind of place Lou'd pick for a holiday. And if he went there for time off, why was he back in Miami, with three paid-up days still to go at this Seaview Motel?"

"I wondered about it," Santini admitted. "So I made a call first thing this morning to the police chief in Coffin City. Man named Hollis Cobb. He said he didn't know anything about any private detective named Lou Kovac. But he promised to ask around and find out if Kovac was working on a job of some kind there." Santini paused and looked at me. "Which he may do. Or he may not."

I narrowed my eyes at Santini. "Meaning which?"

"Meaning he'll do it if it suits him to. He won't if he's got any reason to hush anything up. I also made another call this morning. To the State Police. According to the cop I talked to, this Police Chief Hollis Cobb is deep in the pocket of Hugh Tallant, the guy who runs the moonshining and everything else that's below-board around Coffin City."

"That's interesting," I said slowly, thinking about it.

"Could be. Or it could be a wrong guess."

"Yeah." I stood up suddenly and headed for the door. When I got it open I looked back at Santini. "I'll be in touch—just in case you dig up anything more. You are going to keep digging into what happened to Lou, aren't you?"

"Sure," Santini said, not hopefully. "But you know how hard it is to nail down any of these professional jobs. The bastards that did this may never be found."

"This time they'll be found," I told Santini, very quietly. "You lay any odds you want on it. *They'll be found.*"

I went down to my Olds and drove away. I considered paying a visit to Lou Kovac's office and apartment. But it would have been waste motion. Art Santini had been to both places. He was too much of a cop to have missed anything.

Instead, I drove south out of Miami to Dinner Key, and walked out along the pier to the *Straight Pass*, a cabin cruiser that served as my home. I got the bottle out of the galley and sat for a time in the cockpit fishing chair, sipping brandy and thinking about Lou Kovac—and Coffin City.

Tangerine, a battle-scarred waterfront tomcat who knew me for a soft touch, prowled down the pier and sprang into the cockpit and eyed me fiercely. After a while I got him a saucer of milk. While he lapped it greedily I went back to sipping brandy in the fishing chair and thinking.

Tangerine finished the milk, gave me a glare that passed for a look of gratitude in his circle, and stalked off along the Dinner Key dock in search of more handouts. I watched till he was out of sight near the big luxury yachts along the first pier. Then I went into the cabin and began getting things out of the locker and stowing them in a suitcase.

The final item I took from the locker was the box containing my newly acquired Luger automatic.

I'd acquired the Luger the same way I'd come by the boat: I'd won it in a crap game. I'd only had the Luger pistol two weeks, but of all the weapons I'd ever used, it was my favorite. I'd sailed out on the Gulf Stream and done some target practice with it against floating objects. The Luger had lived up to its reputation, fitting my hand so naturally that it seemed to aim itself. All I'd had to do was point it at a target, as easily as I'd point my finger. What the Luger was pointed at, it hit.

I loaded it and slipped it into its soft kid holster and hooked the holster to my belt under my jacket. Putting two extra clips of ammo in under my shirts, I closed the suitcase, carried it with me back to my car, and drove north to Coffin City.

Chapter 2

IT WAS LATE AFTERNOON WHEN I DROVE INTO COFFIN CITY along a new-made highway that followed the beach. There was a mammoth floating dredge at work filling in a stretch of coastal marshes with bottom sand. Farther on, construction crews were erecting small ranch houses on land already filled in. Beyond, the highway cut through a completed and inhabited development grouped around a gigantic supermarket, the houses as alike as so many cubes of sugar dipped in pastel and fringed with green. The highway went on past a strip of big luxury homes, open to beach and sea, but shielded from the highway by estate walls dripping with frangipani, hibiscus and poinsettias, and well-tended stands of banyan, fig and palm trees. After that, I was in the older center of Coffin City.

It was an off-white town with wide, dusty streets drenched in sunshine and black patches of shade under striped awnings. Its heart was three close-packed blocks of weather-beaten hotels, boarding houses, stores and gin mills. Most of the town seemed to be sensibly lying in wait for sundown. But there were already some people getting a head start on the evening, pushing slowly through the heat between booze joints.

Getting directions at a store where I bought a pack of cigarettes, I drove down to a dock area crowded with fishing-supply shops and boats, cut right and went north out of the center of town to a long row of newish motels between the beach and the road.

The Seaview Motel was a fairly modern-looking place built in a big U around a parking area and swimming pool. I parked and climbed out and stretched myself, loosening some of the stiffness of the long drive. There was the usual amazing variety of swimsuits, shapes and sunburns scattered around the pool. The only ones in the pool were a young, skinny lifeguard and a plump, pretty girl. They were in the shallow end, and he was teaching her the Australian crawl. She wasn't learning much, and she wasn't likely to, the way he was holding her. But it seemed to satisfy both of them. I dragged my suitcase from the back seat of the Olds and lugged it toward the entrance lobby.

Across from the lobby shrill laughter and chatter issued from the doorway of a dim bar. The lobby itself echoed with gunshots from a television set against the left wall. The room clerk was all alone in there, leaning an elbow on the registration counter and watching the western on the TV screen. He didn't look up when I came in.

I rapped my knuckles on the counter beside him. He fixed the progress of the plot in his mind before tearing his gaze from the screen and looking up at me. He was young, with one of those pleasant, polite and pointless faces that seemed to be the style with a generation that accepted the safety of being noncommittal and was coming to accept the probability of non-survival.

"Yes, sir?" he said with a deep drawl. "Have you a reservation?"

"Do I need one?"

He gave me a smile that meant nothing and cost nothing. "All our rooms have been booked well in advance, sir. You might try farther down the road, at . . ."

"A friend of mine is registered here. Louis Kovac."

"Kovac—" His slight frown was as meaningless as his smile. "Oh, yes. Room twelve. But I'm afraid he's not in at the moment. He went out yesterday morning and hasn't come back yet.''

"He won't be back. He's had an accident. Didn't the police tell you?''

"Police?'' He looked puzzled.

"Haven't the police been here today, asking about Mr. Kovac?''

"No, sir. There's been no one in asking about Mr. Kovac. Why? Is he badly hurt?''

"Yes. Badly.'' I took a ten-dollar bill from my pocket and put it on the counter in front of him. "He's registered to the end of the week. Any objection to my using his room for the rest of his paid-up time?''

He looked down at the bill and up at me, still puzzled. "Well, I don't know about that, sir.''

"I can square it with the manager, if you'd rather.''

"The manager is away. There's just me and the night man in charge, till he gets back.''

"Then it's just between you and me.'' I put a five on top of the ten, crosswise. "No sense in the room staying empty for three days, is there?''

The room clerk studied the fifteen dollars, not touching it, waging a small tug of war with his conscience or his fear of sticking his neck out. "But suppose you're wrong? Suppose Mr. Kovac returns.''

"He won't,'' I assured him. "He's in a hospital in Miami. For a long stay.''

The room clerk managed a look of concern. "What in the world happened to him? Was he run over or something?''

"Or something.'' I nudged the two bills against his hand with my forefinger. "Did you say room twelve?''

"Yes, I . . .'' He studied the fifteen dollars some more, then picked it up and stuffed it in his pocket and got the key to room twelve from a pigeonhole behind him.

The exchange of money changed our relationship. "How

long ago did Mr. Kovac register in?'' I asked flatly as I took the key.

"Ah—almost two weeks ago.'' He still looked worried, but the situation was beyond reversing now.

"Who made the reservation for him? Mr. Kovac himself, or someone else?''

"Mr. Kovac did. He sent a note and a check, one week in advance.''

"He have anyone meet him here? Any visitors?''

"No. Not any that I saw. He was hardly ever here himself.''

"He make or get any phone calls?''

The room clerk shook his head. "Not while I was on. I *could* ask our night man, when he comes on.'' There was a look in his eyes that told me his greed had won the battle with his worry.

"Do that,'' I told him. "Mr. Kovac was doing business with someone in this town. Find out who it was and there's another ten for you.'' I picked up my suitcase. "Where's room twelve?''

He pointed through the windows. "Over there, to the left of the pool, the third door from the beach. Would you like some help with your bag, sir?''

"I can manage the bag. You concentrate on finding out who Kovac had contact with while he was staying here. If there are any calls, my name's Rome.'' I lugged the suitcase out of the lobby and down past the pool to room twelve.

It was a fairly spacious room, with floor to ceiling louver windows and a double bed. The furniture wasn't more than a year old, but already showed signs of taking a beating. There was a gray wash 'n' wear suit and a suitcase that belonged to Lou Kovac in the closet. I opened the suitcase on the bed. It contained spare socks, shirts, handkerchiefs, underwear. There was a pair of Lou's shoes under the bed. He'd expected to return.

I searched his suit and suitcase, and then the rest of the

bedroom and the bathroom, without finding anything that was the slightest help to me. Leaving the room, I got directions from the room clerk and drove to Town Hall for a talk with Hollis Cobb, Coffin City's Chief of Police.

He was a stocky man somewhere in his forties, with meaty shoulders and a solid paunch. His hard, lumpy face had small, suspicious eyes and a thin, vicious mouth. He stood in front of his desk, his feet planted slightly apart, his hands shoved deep in the pockets of his brown trousers. He eyed me with belligerent impatience as I came in. His police chief's badge was prominently displayed on the lapel of his jacket and a Colt .45 revolver bulked large on his hip.

"Well?" he grated at me. "What is it?"

"My name's Rome," I told him. "Anthony Rome. I'm a private detective. From Miami."

"Sergeant Gruder already gave me that on the phone. What do you want? And make it quick. I'm already two hours late for dinner."

His office was big, with white-washed walls, high ceilings and seedy furniture that might have been picked up at a rummage sale. The tall windows were closed, and an air-conditioner worked noisily in one of them. After the heat outside, the room felt like the inside of a meat locker. In back of the police chief, on the wall behind his desk, was a big poster with a blown-up picture of his face on it. He was grinning in the picture, and didn't look unpleasant at all. Under the picture it said:

Elect Experience
HOLLIS COBB
KNOWS THE JOB

I'd seen two more posters like it on telephone poles outside the Town Hall. I asked him, "When's the election?"

It startled Cobb a bit. "End of the month. Why? What's it to you?"

"Nothing, I guess. I'm here about Lou Kovac. Lieutenant Santini of Miami Homicide phoned you about what happened to him this morning."

His suspicious little eyes stayed on my face, very steady. "How's it concern you?"

"Kovac is a friend of mine. I'm trying to find out who did it to him. And why."

"Looking in the wrong place, ain't you? He got himself beat up in Miami, not here."

"Lieutenant Santini and I had a feeling he might've been working on a job here, gotten in somebody's hair. Somebody who had him trailed back to Miami and put out of action there."

"Well, you were both wrong," Cobb stated flatly. "You could've saved yourself the trip. I called Lieutenant Santini four hours ago and told him. Kovac wasn't here on any job. He was just having himself a little fun and relaxation. I checked and made sure of that."

"That's mighty fast checking," I said. "Even for a town this size."

His eyes got smaller, but his voice didn't change. "I didn't have to check the whole town. Found out all I needed to know at his motel."

"You've been there," I said with no particular intonation.

"Of course. Manager says Kovac spent almost every minute of his time there. Laying around in the sun, swimming in the pool, drinking in the bar. Nights, some woman came around and shacked up with him in his room." Cobb's lumpy face manufactured a grin. It wasn't as good as the grin on the poster. "This is a town for a man to have a good time in. That's what Kovac was doing here. Having himself a good time. Nothing else."

"This woman you say spent her nights with Kovac—who is she?"

Cobb shrugged his meaty shoulders. "From the little description I got, she could be any one of a hundred in-and-out tourists that hit this town. Probably just a dame from one of the other motels that he met on the beach, here for a good time just like Kovac.''

"Kovac left with three paid-up days still to go at his motel. Funny thing for a man on a vacation to do.''

Cobb shrugged again. "Maybe the dame he was shacking with went to Miami and he decided to go with her.''

I said, "Uh-huh," and stood there thinking about why he was lying to me.

"So you see," Cobb said, "you wasted your time coming all the way over here. If you want to tag whoever hurt your Mr. Kovac, the best thing for you to do is turn around and head back to Miami.''

We looked at each other. I said quietly, "No, I don't think I'll do that just yet. First I think I'll nose around your town a bit. Do some checking of my own. If you don't mind.''

Cobb's face reddened. He took his hands out of his pockets. They were large hands. He squeezed them into fists. "Meaning you think I've been lying to you?" he asked softly.

"Meaning Lou Kovac is a close personal friend of mine. So I want to be absolutely sure. Of everything.''

Hollis Cobb was the kind of man who couldn't hold in tension very long without letting off some of it through physical action. He didn't want to hit me, maybe because election time was too close and he wasn't sure if I had political weight or not. So he stalked from his desk to one of the windows and stood staring through it, drumming his thick fingers on the wall.

Finally he turned around and growled. "You'd better head back for Miami. Don't take your time about it.''

I raised an eyebrow at him. "You kicking me out of your town, Chief?''

"No," he said, getting his voice under control. "I'm just giving you a piece of friendly advice. This isn't your territory.''

"My license is good all over the state. Coffin City is still part of the State of Florida, isn't it?"

"I'm not talking about your license, Rome. I'm talking about how a guy can walk real heavy in his own territory, where he's got friends and big contacts and strings to pull. But if he goes out of his territory, where he don't know anybody, and tries the same stuff, he might just as well cut his own throat. Maybe you're a wheel in Miami. This ain't Miami. You don't know anybody here."

"I know you."

Cobb made an exasperated gesture with his hands. "I can't be every place at the same time. I keep the lid on pretty good. But a good-time town like this—there's bound to be some rough characters in it. You starting nosing around, it could make some of 'em nervous. You can't count on my being right on the spot to help if you fall into a load of grief."

"Thanks for the advice," I told him. "I'll be going now."

"Back to Miami?"

"Eventually." I went to the door. "Good luck in the election." He was moving toward his desk as I went out.

I left with the knowledge that my trip to Coffin City hadn't been a waste of time. Chief Cobb had lied about checking with Lou Kovac's motel, which made the rest of what he'd told me lies too. There could be only one reason why he hadn't bothered to check on Lou after Santini's phone call. He'd already known about Lou. And he was obviously anxious to bury what he knew. I'd come to the right place. Whatever Lou had gotten himself into, it had originated here.

My Olds was parked in front of the Town Hall. I got in and started the motor. A short, fat man in a rumpled white suit came out of the Town Hall entrance and stood on the steps, studying me and my car.

I turned my head and met his stare with one of my own. He gave me a cherubic smile and didn't look away. I put the car in gear and drove off up the street.

Three blocks farther along, I passed a blacked store front

with the sign *Coffin City Clarion* on it. Slowing, I thought about it. When I came to an open spot at the curb I pulled into it, got out of the car, and walked back.

There was a high counter just inside the *Clarion*'s door, and a small, dark old woman behind it.

"This a daily or a weekly paper?" I asked her.

"Weekly." She looked me over curiously, trying to decide how in the world I could have been so ignorant of what everyone knew.

"When do you come out?"

"Tomorrow," she told me. "If you'd like a copy of our *last* edition, I can . . ."

"No. Is there a daily paper in this area?"

"This is the *only* paper. If you are interested, we may be going daily before too long."

I told her I wanted to place an ad in the next edition, and she pushed a sheet of paper and a pencil across the counter to me. "Please *print*."

I printed: ANYONE WITH INFORMATION ABOUT LOUIS KOVAC MAY FIND IT WORTHWHILE TO GET IN TOUCH WITH ANTHONY ROME AT THE SEAVIEW MOTEL. KOVAC HAS MET WITH AN ACCIDENT. HIS ASSIGNMENT WILL BE COMPLETED BY ROME.

The woman behind the counter tallied up the number of words without reading them, and told me how much I owed. I paid her and went out.

The short, fat man was across the street, seated behind the wheel of a black Ford sedan. On the door of the sedan was painted: COFFIN CITY POLICE DEPARTMENT.

We gazed across the street at each other. He gave me another cherubic smile. I walked to the end of the block and went into a diner and had a fish dinner that turned out to be as good as any I'd ever eaten. When I came out of the diner it was getting dark. The few street lamps had gone on. Red, blue and yellow neons were flashing. The pavements were crowding up, the joints were turning noisy.

The fat man with the cherubic smile wasn't anywhere in sight. It seemed to be the right moment to go back to the motel, get some rest, and find out if someone else was ready to make the next move.

Someone was.

Chapter 3

THE CURTAINS OF ROOM TWELVE WERE CLOSED AND LIGHT showed behind them. I saw that as I pulled into the Seaview Motel's parking area. Switching off motor and headlights, I sat there watching. I hadn't shut the curtains before leaving, and I hadn't left the lights on.

Underwater lighting cast a pale blue glow around the swimming pool. There was no one in it and the terrace around it was deserted except for the palm trees and beach chairs. The muffled sounds of liquored voices and a three-piece band came from the motel bar behind me. The palm-shadowed walk that ran past room twelve seemed deserted.

A single shadow moved briefly between the light inside the room and the drawn curtains, then vanished. The door did not open. I got out of my car and drew the Luger from the holster. Holding it down against my leg, I walked toward room twelve, my movements slow, quiet and tensed.

At the door I paused, putting an ear to the upper panel. I listened for several minutes without hearing anything. Getting the key from my pocket with my left hand, I inserted it in the lock, taking infinite care to make no sound. When it was all the way in I took a deep breath and brought the Luger up waist high. Then I turned the key and shoved the door open in the same motion and took a fast, long stride into the room.

The door banged against the interior wall. There was nobody behind it. From where I stood I could see the inside of the bathroom. Nobody was in there, or in the open closet. The only one in the room was a tallish girl in her early twenties, standing beside the bed. Kovac's suitcase and my own were open on the bed, and she was going through mine. The two spare cartridge clips were in her hands when I broke in on her. She dropped them and twisted in my direction, going rigid with terror at the sight of the Luger in my hand.

Her silky, wheat-colored hair framed a healthy, clean-cut young face with a snub nose and wide brown eyes. Freckles showed through her golden tan. Her green dress fitted her loosely but not too loosely. She was a long-legged, high-hipped girl, with a strong, slender waist and marvelous breasts. Her figure still retained a touch of youthful plumpness. Just a touch. The fashion magazines would disapprove, but a man wouldn't.

I shut the door behind me. "I live here. What's your excuse?"

She didn't answer. She wasn't even looking at me. All she could see was the gun pointing her way. I put it back in its holster and buttoned my jacket so she couldn't see it any more. After a moment she relaxed enough to look at me. Something she saw seemed to reassure her. Her look of fear began to change to one of acute embarrassment.

"I . . . I'm sorry," she said shakily. "That . . . Are you Anthony Rome?"

"Uh-huh."

"That ad you put in the *Clarion* . . . I tried to phone you. Twice. You didn't answer, so I finally came here. The room clerk said you were out. So . . ." Her face acquired some pink under the tan and she didn't finish.

"So you broke in and started going through my things."

"Yes. I . . . I've never done anything like this before," she finished lamely. She clasped her hands behind her and looked down at the carpet like a schoolgirl.

"You must be playing beginner's luck. How'd you manage to get in?"

"The window. One edge of it is quite close to the door. The louvers are wide open. I just reached through and turned the inside knob." She sounded a little proud of herself, along with the embarrassment.

I glanced behind me. The edge of the window *was* close enough to the door for her to have done it that way. It was something to remember.

I looked back to her. "The *Clarion* doesn't come out till tomorrow. How do you know about the ad?"

She raised her eyes to mine. "I'm Serena Ferguson. I'm the editor of the *Clarion*. The woman who took your ad gave it to me as a matter of course."

"You're pretty young to be running a newspaper. Even a weekly. You own it?"

"My brother owns it. And I'm not so young. I graduated from journalism school at Northwestern two years ago." Her look defied me to say that didn't entitle her to consider herself a veteran newspaperwoman.

"Good for you. But that doesn't explain what you're doing in my room, searching my things."

"I . . . Your ad was so strange . . . It naturally made me curious."

"Baloney. It wouldn't make you curious enough to risk a charge of breaking-and-entering. What's your connection with Lou Kovac?"

"What's *yours*?"

"I'm a Miami private detective. Like Kovac. I've known him all my life. In fact, he's my godfather. Connection enough?"

She studied me, thinking hard. Then she asked, "Do you mind if I sit down? My legs are kind of shaky."

"Go ahead."

She sat on a chair beside the bed. Her green handbag was on the night table. She picked it up and put it on her lap, grasping it with both hands. Sitting down seemed to give her confidence. Or something did.

She said, "Your ad reads that Mr. Kovac has met with an accident. What does that mean, exactly?"

I told her, in detail. She began to look sick.

"Is that really true?" she whispered weakly. "Or are you making it up to . . ."

I gave her the name of the Miami hospital. "You can phone them and ask easily enough." I moved closer, looking down at her. "Your turn now. Are you the one Kovac was working for?"

"No . . ." She hesitated, taking her lower lip between even white teeth. It was a full, delicious-looking lip, well worth nibbling.

She let the lip go and said, "The rest of your ad—about completing Mr. Kovac's assignment. What does that mean?"

"It means I'll do anything that'll lead me to the men who did the smash job on Lou Kovac. Now how about opening up? You're staying here till you tell me what you know. Make up your mind to that."

"But how do I know you're what you say you are?" she demanded, polite but troubled. "How do I know you're not really working for . . . for *them* "

"Who are *them*?"

She went on looking at me, not answering.

I sighed and told her, "You can check on me by calling Art Santini in Miami. He's a lieutenant with the homicide bureau. He'll be off duty now, but headquarters can give you his home number. Just so you'll be sure it is a cop you're talking to. Santini can give you what you want to know."

She thought about it. I nodded at the phone. "You can make the call right now. And while you're at it, I'll make sure *you're* what you claim to be." I pointed to the green handbag on her lap.

She thought some more. "All right," she whispered nervously. She unsnapped the handbag and took out a short-barreled .32 revolver and aimed it at my stomach.

I could have kicked myself. But she hadn't looked like the kind of girl who went around carrying a gun. She still didn't. She was as frightened by what she was doing as I was. Which frightened me still more.

"Keep your finger off the trigger," I instructed her firmly. "Some of those things go off too easily."

"Please . . ." she whispered. "Get away from me and let me go." Her face was pleading. The little .32 trembled in her hand.

I backed away to the wall farthest from the door. She stood up with the handbag clutched in one hand and the gun in her other. Watching me with wide, frightened eyes, she edged sideways toward the door.

When she reached it she said, "I . . . have to make those calls. And see . . . somebody I—maybe I'll be back."

"Any time," I told her through stiff lips. "It's been such a pleasure."

She fumbled at the knob with the hand holding the green handbag, finally got the door open. She went out, slamming the door shut behind her. I heard her heels going by outside. She was running.

I switched off the lights, opened the door and dodged outside. She was already at the parking area. I went after her, but sticking to the shadows and not moving too fast. I still wasn't sure what she was or how nervous she could be. I didn't want her sending any wild shots back in my direction.

She jumped into a Plymouth convertible and gunned it out of the parking area, through the driveway that ran between the motel's lobby and bar. She cut left onto the road and was gone. I'd gotten some of her license number, but not all of it.

I let my breath out slow and walked to the lobby. The room clerk I'd dealt with before wasn't there. The night man was on, totaling bills on an adding machine behind the counter.

He was a short, squat old man with the perpetually tired, put-upon face worn by most nighthawks—from the counter-men in all-night diners to night watchmen and elevator operators.

"My name's Rome," I told him. "I've taken on room twelve."

"Oh—yeah, Eddie told me about that. Eddie's the day man." His ingratiating smile said that Eddie had also told him about the fifteen bucks.

"Eddie leave any message for me?"

"Nope. He asked me what you wanted to know, but I said I couldn't tell him anything." His smile got wider and his eyes went sly.

"Meaning you have something you'd rather give to me in person?"

He nodded, pleased with my cleverness. "Sure. Eddie already got his dough. Why should I share what's coming to me with him? He gets paid more'n I do and that ain't right. I'm the one takes the chance of some bum walkin' in here some night and knocking me on the head so's he can rob the till."

"So tell me," I snapped impatiently.

"Sure—sure. Well, Kovac didn't meet anybody here. And he didn't make or get any calls." He paused dramatically before finishing it: "Except once. He made a long-distance call to New York, early one evening. The same number called him back about two hours later. That was three nights ago."

"Got this New York number?"

"Yep. We always clip extras like that on the bill, to be paid at the end of the week or whenever a guest leaves." The old man reached under the counter where he'd had it waiting, and passed me over a yellow slip of paper with a phone number on it.

I glanced at it, dug in my pocket and dropped a ten-dollar bill on the counter between us. The old man took it but looked hurt. "You gave Eddie *fifteen*."

I got out another five and held it for him to see. "You happen to know what Kovac talked about with this New York number?"

It was a struggle, but he decided against lying. "No. I didn't listen in. Didn't know it'd be important."

"Kovac ever have any woman spend the night with him in his room?"

"Him? Naw. He'd be out most of the night, every night. Get back 'round three or four in the morning. Alone."

I dropped the five. He scooped it up and put it and the ten in his pocket with a sigh of relief.

"Did a young woman come around asking for me this evening?" I asked him.

"Yeah—Serena Ferguson. Told her you was out."

"You know her?"

"Most everybody does. She's always around asking what's been going on, looking for news for that paper of hers. The *Clarion*. She runs it."

"I understand her brother owns the paper."

"Monte Ferguson. Yeah, he owns it."

"If his sister Serena runs it, what does he do?"

"Oh, he's busy with real estate. This is a boomin' place, you know."

I got out another five and traded it to him for a roll of quarters. He'd given me enough warning that he wasn't above listening in on phone calls. I went down the road to another motel and used its lobby phone booth. Half my quarters got me the New York phone number on the yellow slip of paper.

A switchboard operator's voice announced in my ear: "Mason Investigations, can I help you?"

Another private eye. "I'd like to speak to Mr. Mason."

"I'm sorry, his office is closed for the night. This is his answering service; would you care to leave a message?"

"I'd like a number where I can reach him right now," I told her. "I've an important assignment for him and it won't wait. If I can't get him, I'll have to get hold of some other agency.''

She gave me his home phone number. I hung up and used the rest of my quarters calling it.

Somewhere in New York a phone was lifted and a man's voice said, ''Yeah?''

''Mason?''

''Uh-huh. Who's this?''

I told him who and what I was. ''Lou Kovac phoned you three nights ago. Since then he's gotten himself beaten up and I'm taking over for him. I'd like to know what the phone call was about.''

''Well . . . I'd have to be sure you're on the up-and-up first.''

I gave him the name of another New York private detective with whom he could check on me. ''Tell him the last time I saw him was when he was down here and I took him out fishing on my boat. He caught a barracuda.'' I gave him my phone number.

I hung up, opened the booth door, and breathed cooler air till Mason called me back.

''Okay,'' Mason said. ''Lou Kovac just wanted me to check out a name for him. Carol Branco. She was supposed to have a big contract to co-star in some new television series for NBC up here. I checked, and NBC never heard of her. Neither did CBS or ABC. I told Kovac. And that's it.''

''All of it? He didn't tell you why he was interested in this Carol Branco, or anything about the job he was on?''

''Nothing else. Just what I told you. Hope it helps.''

I thanked him, hung up and went out of the lobby. I had a name now. Carol Branco. I also had the girl-editor of the town's only newspaper interested in me and the Chief of Police sore at me—and both of them for some reason scared of me. It was a start.

Returning to the Seaview Motel, I went through the drive-way past the lobby, thinking of taking a drive instead of a rest. As I approached the parking area I was neatly outlined against the lighted lobby windows.

A gun made a very loud noise.

I was too taken up with the sudden searing pain across my left bicep to tell where the gun was firing from. I fell sideways against the back of a car. The fall made the second shot miss me by inches and clang off the car.

The third bullet hit me in the head and knocked me backward through a whirling tunnel ablaze with flashing lights and dripping blood. From there the route was downward—into darkness.

Chapter 4

I HAD THE SENSATION OF HAVING OVERSLEPT AND MISSED some appointment or other. It was real enough to bring me up from the darkness. Memory returned with consciousness, and suddenly I didn't mind at all not having kept that appointment. It had been with death.

I opened my eyes and sat up. The sitting-up part was a mistake. A small bomb went off inside my head. I fell back on a soft pillow, squeezing my eyes shut and and gritting my teeth.

Someone laughed, low and amused.

I waited till the pain ebbed. This time when I opened my eyes I kept my head where it was. I lay on a quilt-covered bed in a small, over-furnished Victorian bedroom. From somewhere in the building came the muffled sound of a band ramming out a Dixieland number. I was stripped to the waist and my shoes were off. The short, fat man in the rumpled white suit stood beside the bed looking down at me. His smile was still cherubic. His pale, tufted eyebrows and unkempt mop of near-platinum hair helped to give him the look of a beardless Santa Claus. A Santa with a deputy police chief's badge on his lapel and a large revolver in a shoulder holster under his jacket.

"Feeling pretty rotten, eh?"

I got my throat cleared enough to say, "Like my head's caved in."

"It ain't. Just creased. You got a hard skull. I'll get you something'll make you feel better." He waddled away from the bed.

I got my right elbow under me and raised myself a bit, carefully, getting my head up this time without any detonation. The fat deputy was at a sink in one corner of the room, filling a glass with water. There was an oval, gold-framed mirror on the wall, and I saw myself in it. There was a lot of surgical gauze wrapped around the upper part of my left arm, and a two-inch bandage taped to the right side of my forehead, just below the hairline. My jacket, shirt and tie were on a chair by a window table. My Luger was in its holster on the table.

The fat deputy came back with the glass of water in one hand and two round white pills on the chubby palm of his other hand. "Here, Doc Kerner said you should take these when you came to. They'll take care of your headache."

I pushed myself carefully to a sitting position and eased my stockinged feet to the Persian carpet. The bomb inside my head sputtered a little, but didn't go off again. I eyed the pills and tried to moisten my lips with a tongue that was just as dry.

"What're you afraid of?" he asked, amused again. "They're only codeine."

I picked the pills off his palm and swallowed them, gulping the water till the glass was empty. He carried the glass to the sink, took a small white envelope from his pocket as he came back to me. "Here's some more of those pills. Doc Kerner left them for you. Said you should take two every four hours till you feel better." He tossed the envelope on the bed beside me. "I'm Luke LaFrance, case you're wondering." He tapped his badge with a short, plump thumb. "Deputy to the Chief of Police, like it says."

"What is this place?" I asked him.

"Algiers Club. Hugh Tallant owns it—and most every

other joint in town. This is his best. And biggest. Almost any kind of activity you're in the mood for downstairs.''

I turned my head slowly, surveying the room. ''And upstairs, too?''

''For them with the yen, sure. There's two more rooms like this one. Man does not live by one vice alone.'' He regarded me with a benevolent twinkle. ''There's some choice goods to choose from, downstairs. In case you're in the mood when you shake that headache. It'll take more dough than you're carrying on you, though.''

''How come I'm here?''

''Hugh Tallant wants a talk with you. He sent me to fetch you. By the time I got there, the motel'd called Doc Kerner and he was there, patching you up. He said you'd be all right—just a creased arm and a nicked skull. So I brought you here to sleep it off.'' He started for the door. ''I'll go tell Hugh you're with us again.''

''Wait a minute.''

LaFrance stopped and turned. ''Yeah?''

''How'd you know I was at the Seaview Motel?''

He gave me another of those smiles. ''Easy as pie. I went into the *Clarion* after you went out.''

''The old lady told you?''

''Didn't have to ask her. Your ad was still on the counter. I had a look at it while she was getting me a back issue. Chief Cobb wanted me to check on your plans, so I went back and told him. We figured I'd better tell Hugh about it, so I came over here and he sent me to get you.''

''That makes three of you that knew where I was staying,'' I lied. There'd been four, if you included Serena Ferguson.

''Yeah. So?''

''So you, Tallant or Cobb could be responsible for that try at knocking me off. Or the three of you together.''

It didn't upset LaFrance in the least. ''Me? I got nothing against you. And if Hugh Tallant wanted you killed he wouldn't have sent me after you so he could talk to you, would he?''

"That leaves your Chief of Police."

LaFrance shook his head. "Cobb doesn't do anything without Hugh's sayso. Anybody'll tell you he's like a puppet on strings. If Hugh doesn't waggle his fingers, Cobb can't dance.''

"Better not let Cobb hear you talking like that, or you'll be out of a job."

LaFrance laughed. "Fat chance. I'm Hugh Tallant's brother-in-law." He opened the door and went out.

A determined effort got me on my feet. The pills were beginning to dull the pain, which helped. I shuffled across the deep pile of the carpet and took my shirt from the back of the chair. The left sleeve had been cut away, probably by the doctor, and the left side of it was soaked with blood. I put it on anyway. It took some doing, with one arm throbbing and going stiff. The bloodied sleeve of my jacket had two small tears—where the slug had gone in and out. I draped the jacket over my shoulders and stuffed my tie in the left-hand pocket. The holstered Luger was still loaded. I fastened it to my belt, far enough back so the fall of my jacket hid it.

When LaFrance came back into the room I was sitting on the edge of the bed, my shoes back on, taking slow drags at a cigarette. Another man came in with him, a tall, very lean man in his late forties. He exuded confidence and controlled impatience. His long face was tough and bony and muscular. Behind steel-rimmed glasses were cold eyes that looked at people the way the eyes of a jeweler appraised flawed gems.

"I'm Hugh Tallant," he announced, the cold eyes going over me. They went from me to the window table, then back to me. He raised his voice and called, "Jesse!"

A big-jawed thug about the right size and age for college football came in. "You want me, Mr. Tallant?"

"Just stay here. And be ready to be useful."

"Sure, Mr. Tallant." Jesse leaned against the wall, folded

his arms across a barrel-chest, and gazed at me incuriously. That put him on one side of me, La France on the other side, and Hugh Tallant in front of me.

"There's three of us," Tallant stated. "And each of us armed—in case you were thinking of starting anything with that Luger."

I crushed the cigarette out in an ash tray on the night table. "I don't intend to start anything. Just want to be sure nobody tries to finish what that gunhawk at the motel botched."

Tallant pulled over a chair, rested a foot on its seat, and leaned an elbow on his raised knee, looking at me thoughtfully. "Meaning you think I had something to do with that? Forget it. If I did, you wouldn't be here. You'd be out in the swamps somewhere, under the mud. Did you see whoever shot at you?"

"No."

"Well—maybe Cobb'll find out. He's out digging around, right now."

"If he hasn't found out anything by tomorrow," I said, "I'll do some digging of my own."

"No, you won't," Tallant told me, slowly and distinctly. "I've got a police force and plenty of men who are on the force to do any kind of work that I think needs being done around here. I don't need help from outside. Maybe you think I do?"

"I wouldn't know, yet."

"I'll *tell* you. I run this town tight and strong. Some people think I run things a little rough sometimes. But that's the only way it can be done. How do you think I've kept the syndicate out? They've been trying to muscle into Coffin City for years. But I've let 'em know this is *my* town, and I've made it stick. Every time the syndicate's tried to get their fingers on this slice of cake I've slapped 'em down. Think that's easy?"

"It takes some doing," I admitted.

"Damn right! And I've done it. I've kept things strictly

local. Fat wallets come here from all over the Gold Coast, to get trimmed in a pleasurable way. I've made sure the dough only flows into *local* pockets.''

"Especially yours," I ventured.

Tallant didn't look angry, just a bit disappointed in me. ''You're all wrong about that. Ask around. Everybody benefits. I *made* this town. Wasn't for me, Coffin City'd still be a two-bit bump along the highway, trying to get along on fines by catching tourists with trick traffic lights and phony speeding violations.''

Tallant took his foot off the chair, put it beside his other on the floor, and stood taller, looking down at me. "The reformers around here just don't understand the way things really are. They forget it was me that made this a rich town. And they figure if I wasn't in control any more, Coffin City would become a Sunday school." He shook his head at the stupidity of people in general. "They couldn't be wronger. This town's too fat a plum to be left alone. They shove me out, and the syndicate will be in like a shot. I'm the only thing that stands between Coffin City and the mobs moving in.''

"All this is very interesting," I told him. "But exactly what has it got to do with me?''

"I just want to know how things are. I've got enough on my mind without you bringing more trouble to my town.''

"I didn't bring it with me. The trouble was here, waiting. I just happened to step on it.''

He went on as though I hadn't spoken: "If I've been able to handle the syndicate, you can see it wouldn't be much effort to handle you—if you start stirring things up. You might as well go back to Miami. You won't do yourself any good here. Either you'll waste your time and other people's money—or you'll finally manage to get in my hair. Which would be your hard luck. Like I said before, there's plenty of swamp out there." He gestured vaguely toward the west. "Nobody'd ever even find your body.''

I drew a slow breath and asked it: "Did you make a speech like this to Kovac?"

Tallant hesitated. Then he nodded. "Yeah. When I found out what he was up to. It was a while before I knew."

"How'd he take it?"

"He left town, didn't he?"

"He intended to come back."

Tallant thought about that. "I don't think so. Kovac didn't look dumb to me."

"He would have come back," I insisted quietly. "Only he got detained in Miami—the hard way."

"Not by me," Tallant said. "Or by anybody working for me. I had no reason to do that to him. He hadn't gotten in my hair yet. Of course if he had, it would have been different."

Tallant wiped his hands together with an air of finality. "Well, that's it. I think you get the message. Now come down and have a drink, on the house. You look like you need one—and a good night's sleep. When you're feeling better tomorrow think over what I said. If you're as bright as you look, you'll go back to Miami."

I stood up. The codeine had taken hold and it didn't hurt at all. There was only the numbness in my brain and some trouble with my balance. I followed Hugh Tallant out of the room. LaFrance and Jesse brought up the rear.

We went down the steps and past a big, noise-jammed gambling room. I had a glimpse of the crowds around the roulette wheels and black-jack tables, and lined up before a wall-long row of slot machines. Farther along the thick-carpeted corridor was the entrance to an even noisier and more crowded night club. The tables were packed and there was a girl on the tiny stage at one end, stripping to the beat of a rock 'n' roll number. We went past, into a small, pleasant, dimly lighted room.

Tallant led me to the bar. "Whatever my friend here wants," he told the bartender. "On the house."

I ordered a double brandy and leaned against the bar, studying Hugh Tallant. "I still don't know exactly why you're so eager to get me out of your town." I made it a question. He looked back at me and didn't answer it.

I tried again: "Aren't you even interested in who smashed Kovac and tried to kill me? Or is it that you already know?"

His face revealed nothing. "I don't know. If it's got anything at all to do with Coffin City I'll find out, sooner or later. Without your help."

My brandy arrived. I gulped down half of it and waited as its blood-quickening heat spread through me.

A girl came up behind Tallant and said softly, "Hi, Hugh. Sorry I'm late."

She couldn't have been more than twenty, but there was nothing youthful about the cynical twist to her long, ripe mouth or the sexual greed in her smoky green eyes. Her face was too small for the mouth and eyes, her ski-tip nose too sharply pointed, her forehead too low. It should have been an ugly face; instead it was strangely exciting. Her figure was slender and wicked in a strapless black evening gown and her shiny black hair flowed in smooth waves to white shoulders, framing her oddly provocative features.

Tallant turned around quickly. I watched what happened to him as he looked at her. His face went soft and the coldness in his eyes dissolved, leaving them the eyes of an aging boy smitten with his first gut-twisting infatuation.

"Val . . ." he said thickly. "I was beginning to think you weren't coming."

"I'm here," she said, in a manner that was somehow contemptuous and eager at the same time.

"Yeah—you sure are." Tallant put his arm around her and led her out of the room, forgetting all about me. Jesse, the young thug with the football build, trailed them at a respectful distance.

"Make a nice couple, don't they," La France said at my elbow.

I turned to look at the fat deputy. "Kind of young for him, isn't she?"

La France grinned. "Hugh's still in his prime. Ain't any reason he shouldn't pick the best stuff around—now Marie's dead."

"Marie?"

"My sister. Hugh's wife, till she took sick and passed on."

"You don't seem terribly cut up about it."

LaFrance shrugged a plump shoulder. "What the hell— Marie's been gone almost a year now." He ordered a beer from the bartender. "Hugh Tallant always was quite a guy with the ladies. In fact, he's quite a guy, period. He can be damn rough sometimes, too, though you mightn't believe it."

"I believe it," I told him. "Wonder how your Police Chief's making out with his investigation?"

"Not so good. Cobb phoned here just before Hugh went up to talk to you. Said he couldn't find anybody that saw the gunman take those pot shots at you."

"How about the slugs he threw at me? There should be three of them lying around somewhere in the motel parking area."

"Cobb found two of 'em. Looked like .38s. He's taking them over to the State Police, but he doesn't figure it'll do much good. Both slugs must've smacked against the car next to you. Got too smashed up for anybody to get ballistics markings off 'em."

His beer arrived and he turned to it. I finished my brandy and trudged out of the place.

A cab took me back to the Seaview Motel. I approached my room a different way this time, walking around the outside of the motel toward the ocean, and doubling back from the beach in the pool area. I almost hoped the gunman would be there again. He wasn't. But the light was on behind the curtains of room twelve again, and the door was partly open.

I pushed it all the way open with the muzzle of the Luger. No one was lying in wait for me. The room was empty. Things were pretty much as I'd left them, but there were small signs that someone had done a search job. It might have been Hollis Cobb, or some of his cops. Whoever it had been, it made up my mind for me. In my dazed, wound-weaked condition, I'd be easy game. In a drugged sleep, I'd be more so. The Seaview Motel was not a good place to spend the rest of the night.

Shutting my suitcase, I lugged it out to my car. My left arm was beginning to hurt again, and there was a dull throbbing behind my eyes. I put the suitcase in the back seat and climbed in the front. I was sliding the key into the ignition lock when the basic instinct to self-preservation rose up out of nowhere and took hold of me. Whoever had tried to kill me probably knew by now that he'd failed. He might not be inclined to leave it at that. Gunning a man down in a thickly populated area at its busiest time of night smacked of over-eagerness born of desperation.

Getting the pencil flashlight from the glove compartment, I climbed wearily out of the Olds. I opened the hood and stabbed the light under it.

The dull throbbing behind my eyes became a sharp, ragged ache. I'd merely been taking a routine precaution. I hadn't actually expected to find anything.

There was a stick of dynamite wired to the ignition circuit.

Chapter 5

WITH FINGERS THAT TREMBLED LIKE HARP STRINGS, I disengaged the dynamite stick from the ignition wiring. I shut the hood, got back in behind the wheel, put the dynamite away in the glove compartment with the flashlight, and leaned back waiting for a wave of dizziness to pass.

The dynamite might not have exploded even if I'd turned the key in the ignition. Perhaps it had been planted there more to warn me than in any serious expectation of its blowing me apart. I was warned. I was scared sick. In my present state it required an enormous effort of will power before I gained some control over the fear pumping through me.

I drove south out of Coffin City. I considered going all the way back to Miami. But less than an hour's driving made me drop the idea. By then my headache had become a malicious crab clamping portions of my brain between its pincers. The pain became almost blinding. I pulled into the next motel I came to, a rundown row of cabins off the highway, and registered under a false name. The sleepy clerk didn't bother to take my license number. I got the brandy-filled hip flask from the glove compartment and carried it in with my suitcase.

Inside my cabin, I locked the door, stuck a chair under the knob, drew the curtains shut. The prescribed four hours between doses of codeine weren't up, but I took two more pills anyway. I washed them down with brandy, snapped off the lights and went to bed, sipping more brandy from the flask until I passed out. It didn't take long.

I dreamed I was looking up at passing faces. Faces that paused and looked down at me before moving on. Art Santini shook his head sadly, his mouth and eyes grim. Hollis Cobb grinned with satisfaction. Hugh Tallant looked down at me with cold eyes and no expression at all. His black-haired young girl friend giggled and pressed slim fingers to her pointy breasts, looking like a Charles Adams ghoul. Luke LaFrance smiled his cherubic smile; he'd grown a white beard, and it turned out he *was* Santa Claus, after all. Serena Ferguson looked a little frightened under her smugness. Lou Kovac shed a tear for me. So did Ingrid Bergman, sensing the long, lonely years ahead of her.

Then the coffin lid came down over me and shut tight. I knocked at the inside of the lid, politely at first, to let them know I wasn't really dead. The lid stayed shut. I pounded harder. It became difficult to breathe as I used up the air inside the coffin. I began banging wildly with both fists, beginning to sweat and yelling as loud as I could but managing to make no sound at all.

I woke up with hot sunlight pressing against the window curtains. My wristwatch informed me that it was almost two in the afternoon. That shocked me off the bed and onto my feet.

My left arm was stiff from shoulder to elbow. My head hurt, but not like the night before. I took two codeine pills, drank three tumblers of water, and put on enough clothes to go out to the roadside diner next to the motel office. Three cups of black coffee later, with the codeine dissolving my headache, I felt a pang of hunger. I fed it with a tough steak, over-fried potatoes and a glass of milk, and returned to my cabin feeling almost myself.

By the time I'd washed, shaved and put on fresh clothing, my mind was functioning constructively. I didn't have all my strength back, but the Luger I strapped on would have to make up for that—if it became necessary. I sat on the edge of the bed and looked at the phone, considering my first move of what remained of the day. There was still fear in me when I thought about Coffin City, but it was a reasoning, sensible fear. The kind that helps you to move through a mine field with special alertness. The panic that had gripped me the night before was gone, giving way to a coldly stubborn anger.

I made my first call to Art Santini in Miami, and asked him about Lou Kovac.

"He's about the same," Santini told me. "Can't talk yet, and it'll be some time before he can. We got a break on the case, though. A cab driver was cruising past Kovac's office building about ten minutes before the prowl car got there and found Kovac. He spotted two men coming out of the alley and hurrying away up the street. Each of 'em was carrying what looked like a baseball bat, and that struck our cab driver as strange so he took a good look."

"*How* good?" I demanded, holding down a quick stab of excitement.

"One was a tall blond with a powerful build. And he had a slight limp. The other man was about average height, slim, dark hair. Both wearing dark, ordinary suits, no hats. They got in a black Buick and drove away. The cab driver didn't make the license."

"Could he identify them if he saw them again?"

"Not so it would stick in court. He didn't see their faces."

"It's enough for you to go hunting on, though," I pointed out, needlessly.

"We're hunting," Santini assured me. "Don't you worry about that. If we find 'em we'll grab 'em. Even if it turns out we can't hold them."

"Just hold them long enough for me to get there," I said harshly. "Then you can let them go."

"Easy, boy," Santini murmured. "Take it easy. . . . How're you making out up there with Coffin City?"

I told him about the attempt to gun me down, and about the dynamite.

Santini whistled softly into the phone. "Doesn't take you long to make an impression, does it? Begins to look like Kovac's trouble did start there. By the way, I had a call last night from some woman up there. Claimed to be editor of the local paper. Asked if you were really Kovac's godson. Since she already seemed to know, from you, I confirmed it. Did I do right?"

"Uh-huh."

"Where's she fit in?"

"I'm about to find out," I told him.

"Be careful, Tony. It might not be a bad idea to let the State Police in on what you're doing. They've been stymied by the Coffin City cops for years. Lieutenant Waine's the guy to contact in that county. If things get too rough for you, he'd love an excuse to throw his state cops into that town."

"I'll keep that in mind," I promised.

I stepped into a supermarket on the outskirts of Coffin City. As I'd hoped, there was a magazine and newspaper rack near the checkout counters. Among the national magazines and Miami and Fort Lauderdale papers I found what I wanted: the *Coffin City Clarion*. I took it back to the car.

My ad requesting information on Lou Kovac was boxed at the bottom of page one. There were no other ads on the page. I leafed through the rest of the paper. Its other seven pages contained plenty of ads, large and small, along with local news and chatter and several syndicated columns that didn't interest me. I went back to the first page.

Near the top was a two-column face-shot of a smiling, handsome man somewhere in his thirties. He had wide-set, careful eyes and high cheekbones, a strong straight nose, and an aggressive strength to his jawline and chin. The smiling mouth was younger than the rest of his face, in some measure justifying his crew-cut. Above his picture it said:

GIL HURLEY FOR CHIEF OF POLICE
A New Broom Sweeps Clean

It was an endorsement, not an advertisement. Under Gil Hurley's picture was an editorial. Northwestern had certainly not taught Serena Ferguson to put editorials on the front page, so it was a case of political conviction overcoming editorial judgment.

According to the editorial, the growing numbers of decent citizens were eager to break Hugh Tallant's vicious hold on their city, and Gilbert Hurley was exactly the right man to do it for them. Tallant had made Coffin City notorious throughout the state as a hotbed of sin and corruption. Tallant-controlled officials and policemen made matters worse by thwarting state attempts to interfere with Tallant-owned establishments: wide-open gambling, moonshine-distribution and prostitution. For a long time Hugh Tallant had fought against the use of unused city land for housing developments, fearing that an influx of honest, God-fearing people would undermine his control of Coffin City politics. In spite of him, new homes *had* been built, and decent citizens *had* moved in.

There were enough of these decent citizens (two words used over and over again in the editorial) now to vote in clean government if they understood the issues involved enough to support the newly formed reform party. Ordinarily they would have to wait another year, till the regular city and county elections. But the unexpected death of Chief of Police Raymond Jones had given them an opportunity to get the ball rolling at the end of the month, when they could elect a new police chief.

Acting Police Chief Cobb's arrogant assertion that he was the right man for the job because of his past experience was poppycock. Gilbert Hurley, as a respected and brilliant lawyer, understood the law better than Cobb. And as an honest, fearless man, Gil Hurley had a desire to *enforce* the law, which Cobb did not. Cobb, having been one of the police chief's deputies before Tallant elevated him to acting police chief, had for years earned his living as the hireling of the corrupt, graft-ridden city administration now in power. A vote for Gil Hurley as the new Police Chief was a vote against Tallant's administration, a vote for clean government, a vote for a city whose citizens could hold up their heads with pride, instead of bowing them in shame. And so on .

The editorial was signed: *Serena Ferguson, Editor-in-Chief*.

I went back into the supermarket and phoned the *Clarion*. The woman who answered told me the editor had gone home for the day. I found Serena's home address in the phone book.

It was on a wide, tree-lined street of big houses set far apart on lawns hidden by solid banks of hedges seven to eight feet high. I slowed as I approached the Ferguson address, then saw something that made me accelerate and drive on past it. There was a black Buick sedan parked in front of Serena Ferguson's hedge.

It didn't have to be the same black Buick as the one used by the two hoods who had given Lou Kovac the beating. There were plenty of black Buicks, even in Florida where most people who could afford them preferred creams and whites and two-tones. But Coffin City was not a town in which it was safe to take chances—no matter how slim.

I parked out of sight around the corner and walked back, extra-conscious of the weight of the Luger on my belt. The black Buick was two years old, had Florida plates and new tires, and there was a golf bag full of clubs in the back seat. Otherwise, it was just a black Buick. It stood in front of an opening in the tall hedge. I went through the opening, walking softly.

There was more hedge inside, flanking a flagstone path that led to a big, solid house built in a style somewhere between neo-plantation and whitewashed Victorian. Round white pillars supported a turreted porch. At the foot of the porch steps stood Serena Ferguson talking to a tall, wide-shouldered man with a crew-cut. They were too engrossed in each other to notice me. And they were too far away for me to hear what they were saying to each other.

The man was turned so that I couldn't see his face. Serena seemed awkward with him. She wore a white blouse and red shorts which displayed her long, shapely legs and full-bodied curves with an arrogance of which she seemed almost unaware.

Apparently the man with her was aware enough for both of them. He suddenly took her shoulders in his hands and pulled her to him. She looked startled, and then her face was hidden by his head as he kissed her mouth. It wasn't a peck. After a moment her hands came up slowly and clawed at his back, forcing him against her more tightly. The next moment she was pushing him away, shaking her head back and forth violently. He let her go and said something. She listened, upset but not angry.

I backed through the hedge opening and walked away up the pavement. At the end of the block I turned and began strolling back. The man who'd kissed Serena came through the hedge and climbed into the Buick. He glanced up, incuriously, as I strolled past. The face that had been on the front page of the *Clarion* belonged to him. Gilbert Hurley, clean-government candidate for Chief of Police.

Behind me, the Buick came to life and drove away. I made another about-turn, went back to the opening in the tall hedge and along the flagstone path toward the house. Serena Ferguson was climbing the steps.

I called out, "Hi, there."

She stopped on the porch and turned quickly, her eyes going wide at the sight of me. "Mr. Rome! Where have you been?"

I climbed out of the blazing sun into the shade of the porch. "Worried about me?"

"I *was*. After I checked with the hospital in Miami and Lieutenant Santini, and talked to my brother, I tried to reach you. I found out about the attempt on your life, and that you were wounded. I was very upset, naturally."

Her wide brown eyes went to the bandage on my forehead. "Is it . . . Are you badly hurt?"

"Nothing that won't heal." She was a disturbing girl to be that close to. It was the thoughtful appraisal in her brown eyes as much as her obvious latent sensuality.

"I found out you'd been taken to the Algiers Club," she said. "I called there, but they said you'd left. I tried calling you at your motel, and then again this morning. When they told me you hadn't been in at all last night, I really began to worry. I was afraid Hugh Tallant might have had you killed. Finally, after trying the motel twice more, I couldn't stand it. So I phoned your Lieutenant Santini again, half an hour ago. When he told me you were still alive, I . . . began to wonder."

"Wonder what?"

She couldn't meet my eyes. "If Tallant had . . . frightened you off. Or . . . ." She sucked that delicious lower lip between her teeth, unable to finish it.

I finished it for her: "Or *bought* me off?"

"I didn't really believe that," she said quickly. Her eyes came up to mine again. "Knowing your relationship with Mr. Kovac—and how determined you must be to see Tallant punished for what he did to Mr. Kovac."

"*Did* Tallant do it?"

"Of course."

"Can you prove it to me?"

"Well—it stands to reason, doesn't it? He must have found out what Mr. Kovac was doing here."

"That's what I came to find out. What *was* he doing here?"

"There's an election coming up at the end of the month, for Police Chief. We—some of the decent, responsible people of Coffin City—have put up Gil Hurley as a candidate for that office. He's a lawyer. An excellent one. And the kind of man who'll clean out the corruption and vice for which our city has become so notorious, and in doing so break Hugh Tallant's vicious control over our city government."

She was beginning to sound like her editorial. I cut in: "How did Lou Kovac picture in all this?"

"He was hired to get provable evidence of how Tallant has corrupted Coffin City. Ammunition I could use in my paper, and Gil could use in his speeches, to make people see the light and vote for Gil—as a vote against Hugh Tallant."

"Did Kovac dig up much dirt for you?"

Serena thought about that. "No—nothing much that we didn't already know. He warned us it might take time to get actual proof—so we wouldn't lay ourselves open to charges of libel and slander. But he must have been just on the verge of finding out something—something big, that would really hurt Tallant. So Tallant had him stopped. Doesn't that stand to reason?"

"It's possible," I conceded. "You said *we* hired Kovac. You and who else?"

"My brother, for one. Which reminds me. Monte's very anxious to meet you, talk to you. Do you mind if I phone him right now, and let him know you're here?"

I curbed my impatience. "All right."

"Would you like something to drink while we're waiting for him?"

I shook my head. "Too early in the day for me. I just got up."

Serena grinned. It was the first time I'd seen her smile. It went well with her clean-cut, healthy good looks. "I meant something like lemonade. Something cool. It's so damn hot today.''

"Lemonade would be fine," I told her.

"You might as well make yourself comfortable out here. The porch is the coolest part of the house during the day." She turned toward the door.

"By the way," I said, "wasn't that Hurley, your candidate for Police Chief, I saw leaving here as I came by?"

She stopped, keeping her back to me for a moment. Then she turned. She met my look directly enough, but there was concealment in the brown depths of her eyes. "Yes. He . . . dropped in for a moment, to . . . thank me for an editorial on the coming election that I put in this morning's issue."

There was nothing wrong in a healthy young man ardently kissing a pretty girl to express his thanks for political favors. I said, "I saw the editorial. And my ad. Thanks for putting it on the front page."

"I hope it will help," Serena said. "Maybe somebody who knows what Mr. Kovac found out about Tallant, or was about to find out, will see the ad and contact you."

"That would help," I agreed. "There was nothing in your paper about the attempt on my life. How come?"

Serena made a face. "I found out about it too late. Your ad was the last thing I managed to squeeze in before we put the issue to bed. That's one of the troubles with a weekly paper. Miss getting it in one issue, and you have to wait a week to get it in the next, by which time it's stale news. I'll be a mighty happy woman when the *Clarion* goes daily."

"When does it?"

"After the election. I've felt for some time that Coffin City's growing population warranted our going daily. Only that costs a lot, and my brother has all his money tied up in real estate now. But if Gil becomes our new Chief of Police, he could gain himself a big political future in this state— based on making the right kind of name for himself by cleaning up Coffin City. All it'd take is enough publicity. And I'll be able to give him that, if the *Clarion* becomes a daily."

"Gil Hurley's going to put up the money to turn your paper into a daily?"

"In a way . . ." She hesitated. "Actually, of course, it's Willa's money. Not that that makes any difference."

"Willa?"

"Gil's wife."

Which put a very different complexion on that kiss.

Chapter 6

ICE CUBES CLINKING AGAINST GLASS HERALDED SERENA'S return. She came out onto the porch with a small tray bearing two tall tumblers of lemonade. She'd accomplished a quick change to a lime-green dress that didn't do much about camouflaging her full-blooded womanliness. I didn't think it was deliberate. She just happened to have a figure that was not easily deemphasized.

"I called Monte—my brother," she said as she sat in one of the wicker chairs. "He's coming right over from his office."

We sipped lemonade, and I admired the length of her legs. Sitting down made her much shorter, and stressed the generous curves of her young body.

She crossed one leg over the other and smoothed the green skirt over dimpled knees. "Why are you looking at me like that, Mr. Rome?"

The answer was obvious, so I growled, "I was wondering if you had that .32 concealed on you somewhere."

She laughed softly, crinkling the corners of her eyes. "Were you thinking of searching me?" Her glance flicked over me, then back to my face. There was nothing coquettish about it—just more of that look of thoughtful appraisal. "You'll have to forgive me for last night. I couldn't be sure you weren't someone working for Hugh Tallant. When I read the ad you'd placed, I tried to get in touch with some of the others. I couldn't reach Gil or Monte or anybody by phone. I got impatient and decided to find out who you were on my own. I took the gun along . . . for protection. Just in case. You understand?''

"Are guns standard equipment for lady editors these days?''

"I got one when we decided to run Gil for Police Chief against Tallant's man. Gil has one, too. The same kind. And Seymour Peck.''

"Who's he?''

"Gil's law partner. He's managing Gil's campaign. It was Peck's idea that we'd better be armed—just in case some of Tallant's thugs tried roughing us up.''

"Have they tried?''

"Not yet.'' Serena seemed a bit disappointed. "I suppose we haven't managed to worry Tallant enough. Perhaps we will, now that you're working for us.'' She gave me a direct look, coloring a little. "I get the feeling that you're very— capable. Even more so than Mr. Kovac.''

"Kovac is . . . was . . . damn good at his work.''

"But you're younger. Perhaps you can help us in ways that he couldn't.''

"If I go to work for you.''

She frowned. "Is there a question about that? I thought you wanted to get back at Tallant for what he did to Mr. Kovac.''

"If he did it.''

"Who else would have had any reason to?''

"I don't know. Yet. Understand this—I'm here for only one purpose. To get my hands on *whoever* is responsible for what happened to Lou Kovac. If I find that doing so involves going up against Tallant, I'll be helping you in the process. If not, Gil Hurley's election campaign is no concern of mine.''

"That suits me fine,'' Serena said. "Because I'm certain Tallant is responsible for Mr. Kovac being in the hospital.''

"If so," I told her, "I'm on your side. Who hired Kovac originally?"

"All of us. Monte and myself. Seymour Peck. Willa and Gil."

"Which of you actually paid him?"

"Willa did. But that doesn't matter."

"It might. How'd she happen to pick Lou Kovac for the job?"

"She didn't. When we all decided to hire a private investigator, Seymour Peck said he knew of one with an excellent reputation. He went to Miami and came back with Mr. Kovac."

I sipped more of the cold lemonade and gazed out at the sun-drenched lawn. "Willa Hurley seems to be the one with the money in this combination. You said it was her money that was going to turn your paper into a daily. Doesn't it also belong to her husband—Gil Hurley?"

"Well—not legally. You see, Willa inherited quite a lot of property from her first husband, John Coffin."

"The man this town's named for?"

"Yes. Mr. Coffin owned most of the land around here. Though he never did anything with it. His income was from patents on inventions used by the oil industry. He was much older than Willa—a widower with a daughter—when they married. She'd been his secretary. The income from his patents ran out. So Willa got together with my brother and began turning the land she'd inherited from Coffin into cash by building housing developments on it."

"How long ago'd Coffin die?"

She thought back. "Oh—about four years ago."

"When'd she marry Hurley?"

She didn't have to do any thinking for that one: "Two years ago. It'll be exactly two years, next month."

"Had they known each other long?"

"Since they were kids. They were in the same class in our local high school."

"Childhood sweethearts?"

"No—nothing like that. At least I don't think so. I was too young then to know either of them. But they never *acted* as though there was anything between them—before John Coffin died. Though of course they saw each other fairly often. Gil and Seymour Peck were Mr. Coffin's lawyers, you see."

She was looking away from me, squinting at the sunlight beyond the porch. A tinge of bitterness crept into her voice. "I suppose when John Coffin died Willa just decided she was too young to spend the rest of her life as a widow. So she looked around for some likely male to keep her from being lonely—and picked Gil."

"Have you known Gil Hurley long?" I asked her gently.

"Since he came back from college." Her voice had become toneless. "Seymour Peck is my brother's lawyer, and Gil became Peck's partner. That's how I got to know him." She stood up abruptly. "Here comes Monte."

I put aside my half-finished lemonade and rose to my feet. The man coming up the flagstone walk was about Serena's height and coloring, in his early forties. He had a lean, hard build and a homely, sensitive, serious face. If you'd had to guess at his occupation, you'd have pegged him as a scholar or a scientist, not a businessman.

"This is Mr. Rome, Monte," Serena told her brother as he climbed to the porch.

Monte Ferguson studied me before speaking. "Serena says you want to go on with Kovac's job for us."

"She was jumping the gun," I told him. "I've just explained that to her. I'm after whoever had Lou Kovac beaten up. So far it seems that Tallant was the only one with a motive. But I don't promise anything—if it doesn't turn out that way."

"Fair enough." Ferguson smiled tightly and held out his hand. "That means you'll wind up working for us, whatever your present intention." His handclasp was firm, without undue pressure. "When we've filled you in on what Kovac was doing, you'll realize we have the same enemy."

He released my hand and told Serena, "Willa's expecting us at her place. I phoned her. And Peck's meeting us there." He glanced back at me. "They want to meet you."

"How about Gil Hurley?"

"I wasn't able to locate him. Probably out somewhere shaking hands."

Serena nodded. "Gil told me he was going to do some door-to-door campaigning this afternoon."

Ferguson looked at his sister again. "When'd he tell you that?"

"A little while ago. He dropped by to thank me for the editorial in the *Clarion*."

Ferguson's smile was gone. "Couldn't he *phone* his thanks to you?"

Serena bit her lip and went down the porch steps, striding toward the hedge opening.

As we followed her, I told Ferguson, "My car's around the corner. If you'll tell me how to get where we're going . . ."

"No need. You can come with us in my car. We'll bring you back."

Serena was waiting for us in the front seat of an open Ford convertible, her face stiff. Her brother got behind the wheel, and I slid in on the other side of her. She stared straight ahead through the windshield as Ferguson drove us away.

After a time Ferguson broke the uncomfortable silence, a bit apologetically: "The trouble with Gil is, he spends too much of his time baby-kissing and shaking hands, leaving the hard, solid work of constructing a solid political base under him to Seymour Peck."

"Gil can't very well expect people to vote for him unless they get a chance to know him, isn't that true?" Serena's voice was angry under its control. "You know as well as I do that Gil's biggest asset is that people take to him quickly."

"Popularity is his middle name," Ferguson admitted grudgingly. "Always has been. Even back in high school he was captain of the football team and voted most popular boy in his class. Getting liked was about all he was very good at, to tell the truth. I was surprised when he managed to get through his college law courses."

"Gil's not dumb," Serena snapped. "If he is, why did Peck take him on as a partner?"

"Favor to Gil's dead father. Didn't you know Gil's father originally set Seymour up in practice?"

"The trouble with you," Serena told him bitingly, "is that you still think Peck should have been the candidate, instead of Gil."

"Seymour is older, has more experience for one thing."

"But Gil is the candidate. Willa decided Gil was the one she wanted to push to the governorship—and you gave in to her. So now you have no right to complain."

Ferguson glanced my way and nudged his sister with his knee. The remainder of the drive was quiet and uninformative.

The Coffin estate consisted of some fifteen acres of classically sculptured lawns and walled gardens that gave utter seclusion to a group of three buildings fronting the sea. Ferguson parked in front of one of the buildings, a six-car garage with servants' quarters above. There were two gardeners at work nearby, one trimming back brilliant-flowered tropical bushes, the other riding a motor mower up and down a vast stretch of lawn that looked like a two-acre green carpet. We walked past a white stone cottage with a red tile roof, went through a series of foliage—enclosed terraces decorated with fountains and statues, and reached the main building.

It was a massive, rambling Mexican-modern house—mellow terra cotta trimmed with white, like icing on a mocha cake. Ferguson led us through a brick-and-shell courtyard to the ocean side of the house, onto a tiled patio wrapped around

a big swimming pool of indefinite shape. The patio was sur-
rounded by palms and ferns growing out of enormous red
clay jars.

A tall palm tree grew out of the middle of the pool, and
there was a girl in the water, swimming around its trunk.
She wore no bathing cap, and her black hair streamed from
her head, gleaming wetly like the wings of a raven caught in
a rainstorm.

A woman in a white tennis outfit with a short skirt was
seated in one of the white wrought-iron chairs by the pool-
side, watching the swimming girl. She stood up quickly as
we appeared, and came to meet us.

Ferguson made the introductions: "Willa Hurley—Anthony
Rome."

She was a lean, nervous type in her mid-thirties, with
black hair cut too short for her sharp features and long jaw.
Large green eyes and a mouth of feminine softness saved her
face from being unattractive.

She looked me up and down slowly, as though examining
the lines of a racing horse. "Well! You're certainly a decided
improvement over Kovac, I'll say *that* for you." She flashed
a smile in Serena's direction. "Agreed?"

Serena's answering smile was a touch inhibited.

Willa Hurley returned her attention to me. "So you want
to take over Kovac's job? I hope you do more to earn your
fee than he did."

"Willa . . ." Ferguson cut in gently. "Rome is a close
friend of Kovac's."

Willa Hurley was instantly contrite. "I am sorry about
what happened to your friend, Mr. Rome. But truth is truth.
Kovac didn't do much for us. Can you?"

She sweetened the question with a pleasant smile. I made
my smile just as pleasant. "I don't know that I intend to
try."

"What Rome means," Ferguson explained quickly, "is
that his main purpose is to avenge Kovac. And he's not quite

convinced as yet that Tallant was behind what happened to Kovac.''

"Oh? Well, then, we'll just have to convince him. But why don't we get relaxed first?'' Willa went to a white wrought-iron table with a glass top and rang the small bell on it.

Within seconds, a Cuban houseboy in a white jacket came out of the house, pushing a liquor cart ahead of him. Willa glanced at me. "What'll you have to drink, Mr.—do you mind if I call you Tony?''

I said I didn't mind. My arm was giving me trouble and the edge of a headache was starting again. I ordered a brandy. We sat down around the table and Willa ordered whisky and soda for herself and Ferguson. Serena asked for a gin and tonic.

"I understand there's been an attempt to kill you already,'' Willa said to me. "Is that why the bandage?''

I nodded. "That's why.''

"Doesn't that convince you?''

"It convinces me that somebody around here doesn't want me to find out why Lou Kovac got the beating.''

The houseboy finished mixing and serving the drinks and went back into the house, leaving the liquor cart behind. I got one of the white pills from my pocket and swallowed it with a sip of brandy.

Willa watched me, frowning. "You say *somebody*. Why? You look quite intelligent to me. Isn't the answer obvious? Tallant had Kovac beaten up to prevent him from digging into his affairs for us.''

"Why would Tallant have needed to do that? You said yourself that Kovac hadn't succeeded in turning up much for you.''

"But isn't it possible that Kovac was *about* to find out something concerning Tallant? Something important?''

"Uh-huh. Quite possible.''

"And now Tallant has tried to kill you, to stop you from

finding it out." Willa gave that a moment's thought. "Under the circumstances, Tony, I don't think that motel in town is a very safe place for you to stay."

"I've been thinking along those lines myself," I conceded wryly.

Her big green eyes probed my face. "How about staying here—in the guest cottage? Nobody would dare come after you here."

"It's an idea." I leaned back and grinned at her. "If you're sure you have enough room."

She didn't take it as a joke. Instead she said rather gloomily. "More than enough. Especially with Gil away campaigning so much of the time. It gets damn lonely around here for me." She looked at Ferguson. "In fact, I sometimes wonder if it was such a good idea to let Gil have a political career."

Monte Ferguson patted her hand. "It's a bit late in the day to be having second thoughts about that, Willa."

The girl who'd been swimming in the pool climbed out and pattered over to us, dripping water across the patio tiles. Her slender figure was wickedly erotic in a tight, knitted red bathing suit. Her wet black hair was plastered to the sides of her oddly attractive, near-ugly face.

"Nothing like a swim to wash out the cobwebs," she said as she reached us. "What is this, some kind of conference?"

It was the girl I'd last seen with Hugh Tallant, at the Algiers Club.

Willa Hurley glanced up at her, then at me. "Meet Valerie—my stepdaughter."

Chapter 7

"THIS IS TONY ROME," WILLA WENT ON, TO HER STEP-daughter. "He's . . . a friend of Monte's. He'll be staying with us awhile."

"Welcome to our humble home, Tony." Valerie started to grin at me, but then narrowed her eyes, trying to remember. "I know it's an old line, and my reputation's lousy enough as it is, but—have I met you somewhere before?"

"Uh-huh. Last night. The Algiers Club."

She was sorry she'd asked.

Willa had turned to stare at her. "What were you doing in the Algiers Club, Val?" Her question had a sharp bite to it.

Valerie made her face as innocent as possible. Which was not very innocent. She didn't risk looking at her stepmother. Her eyes stayed on me as she answered carelessly, "I just stopped in a minute for a quick drink."

She continued to watch me, waiting for me to say something. When I didn't, she looked puzzled.

"But why the *Algiers* Club?" Willa demanded.

Valeria shrugged her smooth white shoulders, making her pointy breasts dance in the clinging wet knitted material that cupped them. "Why not? It has a bar, and I was thirsty."

Ferguson chided her with near-paternal concern: "You know you shouldn't go there, Valerie. That was very foolish of you."

By then she'd decided I wasn't going to squeal on her. She

gave Ferguson a crooked gamin-grin. "Why not, Monte? Afraid Hugh Tallant'll kidnap me or something?"

"It's not funny, Val," Willa snapped. "You know how things are now between us and Tallant. And by the way—just when did you get in last night?"

"Search me. I didn't look at the clock."

"It must have been very late. I didn't hear you. Where were you?"

Valerie shrugged again. "Around. I ran into some friends. We put together a little party."

"What kind of party?"

"For God's sake, Willa," Valerie sulked. "Just a *party*."

Willa was studying her, worried. "I hope you're not letting yourself get wild again, Val. You know I've warned you about that. So has Gil."

"He sure has," Valerie snarled. "That's all I ever hear from him any more."

"Naturally he's worried, Val. If you get into trouble again, it won't help his chances."

"That'd be just too bad. . . . Who does Hurley think he is, telling me what to do? He's not my father."

"And I'm not actually your mother," Willa reminded her gently.

Valerie met Willa's look directly for the first time. "That's different. I like you, and you like me. So you've got a right to say whatever you want to me—even things I don't like to hear. But from Hurley I won't take a thing; not even the time of day!"

She flung me a quick last look, still puzzled. Then she stalked off into the house, her bare feet slapping on the tiles and her saucy buttocks twitching with each step.

Serena had both hands flat on the table and was gazing down at them, pretending she hadn't heard any of it. Ferguson was patting Willa's arm soothingly again. Willa continued to look toward the house for a moment, then looked at me and forced a slight smile. "Sorry for the family squabble. But Val can be a handful sometimes."

They all looked relieved when a short, thin man of about fifty came through the courtyard onto the terrace. He came toward us with a quick, efficient stride. He had a florid, no-nonsense face under a thinning tangle of reddish hair.

Ferguson stood up and shook hands with him. "About time you got here, Seymour." He gestured at me. "This is Rome."

Seymour Peck examined me clinically as he stuck out his hand. His handshake was brief and damp. He examined me some more and finally conceded, "He looks capable enough"—as though I were a car he was considering buying.

I took a swig of brandy and drummed my fingers on the table.

Peck seated himself stiffly on the edge of a chair. He leaned toward me almost accusingly, and snapped, "All right. What do you propose to do first?"

I drummed my fingertips a couple more times. "I propose to ask some questions. I'd prefer it if all of you were here to supply answers. But it seems we'll have to do without Hurley for the time being."

Peck looked at Willa. "Where is Gil?"

"I don't know. Off somewhere being persuasive with voters, I suppose."

"He was supposed to drop by the office this afternoon," Peck told her angrily. "He didn't. He's always off someplace, leaving me to do the hard work of this campaign myself."

"Gil does his share." Willa's voice had a hard, sharp quality that flustered Peck. He looked down at his fingers gripping his sharp knees. Willa looked at me and said, more pleasantly, "Gil's bound to be back for dinner. You will be having dinner with us, won't you, Tony?"

"Depends. I have a couple phone calls to make. If I get a lead from one of them, I'll do some moving around. I can't predict when I'll get back."

"But you will be staying with us, while you're here."

I hesitated, thinking it over. "Probably."

Willa smiled. "I'll have a room ready for you, in the guest house."

Seymour Peck looked up at me, a bit subdued. "I'm a busy man, Rome. I came over to have a look at you, and I'm satisfied with what I see. Now, if you'll ask your questions, so I can get back to work . . ."

I finished my brandy and pushed the snifter aside, feeling better. The codeine was on the job again. "I understand you're the one who actually hired Lou Kovac. How'd you come to pick Lou for the job?"

"Harry Chandler recommended Kovac to me." Chandler was a Miami lawyer for whom both Kovac and I had worked on various occasions. "As a matter of fact, I phoned him again this morning, to check on *you*."

"What'd Chandler tell you?"

"He said you were experienced and dependable."

"So was Lou Kovac," I said. "Too experienced to get careless enough for some hoods to get their mitts on him— if he knew he was stepping on a racketeer's toes. Yet that's what you all seem to think happened. That he became a threat to Tallant, and got squashed for it."

"Obviously," Peck stated.

"It's not obvious to me. If Lou had known he was squeezing Tallant where it hurt, he'd have been more careful."

"Kovac isn't as young as you, remember," Ferguson pointed out. "Sometimes even the best of men get careless, as they grow older."

That could explain it, I knew. But I didn't like it that way. "Exactly what had Lou Kovac done that would get Tallant that excited?"

Ferguson shook his head. "I don't know." He looked at the others. They didn't seem to know, either.

"Didn't he dig up anything for you?"

"Kovac found out that some of Tallant's gambling places

were cheating people," Serena said. "And he had an idea that some of the—girls—were being used to blackmail wealthy men who came here to be with them. But he didn't have proof, and we couldn't say things like that without proof. The only thing he got for us that we were able to use was a detailed list of every gambling place in town—and all the places of prostitution. I printed that list in the *Clarion*, although Kovac didn't think it would mean much. He said he'd just made that list as a basis for him to operate from."

"How'd Tallant react to your printing the list?"

"He phoned Serena," Peck said bitterly, "to thank her for the free advertising."

"I see." I leaned back and looked at the four of them—Serena and Willa; Ferguson and Peck. "So where does that leave your theory that Kovac got smashed for bothering Tallant?"

"Isn't it probable," Peck said, "that Kovac had found out something which he hadn't gotten around to telling us—and that Tallant got wind of it? That seems to me to be a fairly elementary deduction."

"Elementary guesswork. Unless he told one of you about this *something*."

"He did mention something to me," Serena said slowly. "The day before he got hurt. Something to the effect that he might soon be earning his keep around here."

I sat up straighter. "That all he said?"

"Yes. I didn't think much of it. I assumed he was just reassuring me that eventually he'd be able to dig up material that would help the campaign. It didn't occur to me that he was referring to anything specific. But now I wonder."

I questioned the others, but if Lou Kovac had been on to anything new, he hadn't told them about it. Ferguson had been the last one to see Kovac, early on the day Kovac had returned to Miami. But Kovac hadn't said anything to him about going to Miami, and none of them had any idea why he'd gone there. Or so they said.

"Could it," I asked softly, "have had anything to do with Carol Branco?"

That seemed to puzzle them. "Carol?" Willa said. "Why are you interested in her?"

"Because Lou Kovac was. I take it you know of her."

"We all do," Serena said. "She's our celebrity. Local girl goes off to the big city and makes good. I did a story about Carol Branco in the paper two issues ago. But what does she have to do with Mr. Kovac?"

"He made a phone call to New York—to get a man there to find out some things about her. The next day he went to Miami—and got put out of action. Any connection?"

Ferguson flicked a worried look at Willa, who sat there looking thoughtful. Her eyes narrowed to slits. I couldn't read them. Peck and Serena just seemed puzzled. No one thought up an answer.

"All right," I said to Serena. "You ran a story on Carol Branco. Tell me about her."

Serena leaned back in her chair and crossed those long, long legs and wrinkled her brow like a lady editor sorting her facts—who, what, where, when, why.

"Carol Branco's a home-town girl. Born and brought up here. Her father was a fisherman, not too successful. He's dead now. Her mother still lives here, works as cashier in one of our movie theaters. Carol had to help out by working as a waitress after school and weekends. In her last year of high school, she was voted prettiest girl in her class. I can understand why. She's still extremely good looking."

"How old?" I asked.

Serena glanced questioningly at Willa Hurley.

"Thirty-three," Willa said in a flat voice. "She was in my class in high school, so she's my age."

"Go on," I told Serena.

"Well—some years after she graduated, she decided to try making a career for herself as a model. She went to Miami first, but from what she told me, she had a difficult time getting started. She was working as a carhop, and taking modeling lessons, when someone told her about the Florida Orange Growers' Association's annual beauty contest. She entered it and won, becoming Miss Florida Orange Juice of the year. That led to an offer of a screen test. She went to Hollywood, but it didn't work out.''

"I could have predicted that,'' Willa said, not quite masking the nastiness of it. "Carol was in a class play, our junior year in high school. She was awful.''

"She told me she did get a few small parts,'' Serena went on, "but they ended up on the cutting room floor. She stayed around Hollywood for a number of years, until she realized she wasn't going to get anywhere unless she learned more about acting. So she went to New York and got work there as a model to pay for acting lessons. Her first break came when she was finally accepted into an acting school with an excellent reputation. That led to work in summer stock, and roles in local television dramas that won her her big break. She's been signed by NBC to co-star in a new network television series. It doesn't start shooting until this spring, so Carol decided to come back here for a month's vacation before starting work.''

"How long ago was this?''

"Uh—almost three weeks now.''

"So she's still here?''

"Yes. I saw her just a few days ago, driving by in that red Jaguar of hers with the silver-blue mink slung over her shoulders.'' Serena laughed. "She certainly came back in style. Exactly like a local-girl-makes-good should come back. It was so perfect I wanted to take a picture of her in that Jag for the *Clarion* story. But she said no—she didn't want that much publicity about her being here; didn't want people bothering her. She came back to get a month's rest in the sun, and because she hadn't seen her mother in almost ten years.''

"The truth is,'' Willa said. "she came back here to gloat. To show off.''

Serena was perplexed by Willa's tone. "She didn't act that way when I interviewed her."

Willa gave a short, unpleasant laugh. "You don't know Carol Branco like I do. She was before your time. I went to school with her, remember. Carol was always that way—always showing off her conquests."

"Conquests?"

"Boys. She used to enjoy taking other girls' boyfriends away from them in school. She got them all—the same way she probably got this television contract."

"She doesn't have any television contract," I said, slowly and distinctly, for effect.

It wasn't exactly a bomb I'd dropped into the conversation. Nobody fell off a chair. But they looked surprised.

"What do you mean?" Serena demanded. "Of course she has a contract. With the NBC network. She told me . . ."

I nodded. "Uh-huh. She told you. It was a lie. Lou Kovac phoned New York and checked on her. NBC doesn't know her. Neither do any of the other networks."

"But why would she lie about it?"

"A good question. Anybody got an answer?"

"It's perfectly simple," Willa said. She looked as happy as a girl with her first evening gown. "Knowing Carol Branco from way back, I'd say she's gotten herself a sugar daddy. And as I told you, she always was a show-off. She decided to come back here with the car and furs and money he gave her, and make a big impression on the old home town by claiming to be a big success in show business."

She giggled, having a fine time. "This is really wonderful! Wait'll I tell Gil." She was going to say more, but suddenly she jumped a little in her chair and shot a startled look at Ferguson. I got the impression he'd kicked her, under the table. It achieved its purpose. She stopped talking.

Peck said irritably, "I still don't understand why Carol Branco's doings would have interested Kovac. Whether she was lying about her career or not. Why would he care? I don't see the connection. Why did he bother to check on her?''

"That's the question." I drew figure eights on the table with my finger and looked at them one by one. None of them had an answer for me.

"Maybe Gil Hurley will be able to tell me," I said, finally.

"What leads you to that conclusion?" Willa demanded stiffly.

I raised and lowered a shoulder. "It's a hope, not a conclusion. I keep asking questions. Eventually, maybe I'll come across somebody with an answer or two." I stood up. "Mind if I use your phone?"

Willa didn't answer immediately. She was looking at me with unfocused eyes, not actually seeing me. Then her eyes focused and she said slowly, "Yes—of course. The nearest one's in the library." She told me how to find the library.

I went into the house, through a huge sitting room done in greens and gold, along a short, wide corridor lined with non-objective paintings, into a room walled from floor to ceiling with bookshelves. The shelves were jammed with books obviously picked for their well-oiled leather bindings. The only justification for the big, dark, ungainly furniture was that the pieces had been looted from some gone-to-seed European estate.

I shut the door and used the phone on the huge oak desk to call the Seaview Motel. I got the day clerk and asked if there'd been any calls for me.

There'd been one, earlier that day, from a woman who hadn't left her name. She had left a message for me, though. The clerk read it over the phone:

"I'll phone you again at six tonight. Be there, if you want to know the truth about what happened to K. Be careful, or the same thing will happen to you."

Chapter 8

I FOUND THE CUBAN HOUSEBOY AND ASKED FOR VALERIE Coffin. But I'd already missed the boat. Willa's stepdaughter had made a quick change and driven off somewhere. She hadn't said where.

Out by the pool, Ferguson was mixing fresh drinks while Serena and Willa argued quietly about what kind of woman Carol Branco actually was. I asked after Peck.

"Had to get back to work," Ferguson said.

"Me, too. Can you drive me?"

Ferguson hesitated, glancing at Willa. "I believe I'll stay here awhile. Serena, do you mind taking Rome to his car?"

Serena didn't mind. She had a last swig at her drink and stood up as Willa asked me, "You'll be back for dinner?"

"I'm afraid not."

"But you will be back, later?"

"You can expect me. For one reason, I want to talk to your husband." I didn't mention her stepdaughter as the other reason.

As Serena drove me away from the Coffin estate she asked, "What do you make of all this, Mr. Rome? I mean—Mr. Kovac's interest in Carol Branco, and her lying about the television contract?"

"Nothing at all," I said, not paying much attention. I was busy thinking.

Serena shot me an incredulous, rather indignant look.

65

"You mean you don't believe it has any bearing on what's happened?"

"An investigator doesn't usually come up with solutions until after he investigates. It's practically a mathematical formula: First the investigation; then the solution."

She didn't take offense. "How do you intend to investigate it?" she asked patiently, like an intelligent pupil prompting a distraught teacher.

"The easy way first. Where do I find Carol Branco?"

She gave me two places to try: Carol Branco's motel, and her mother's home. "Can I come along with you?"

"No. You stay far away from Carol Branco. For a while at least."

Serena smiled sideways at me. "I wouldn't interfere. I only thought it might be educational to watch how a private detective works."

"It could be fatal, too. Somebody's gunning for me, remember? He might not mind blasting you along with me, if the occasion arose."

"Oh." She thought about that for a time. Then she glanced my way again. "The prospect doesn't seem to frighten *you* much."

"The hell it doesn't. . . . That was an odd exchange between Willa Hurley and her stepdaughter, back there by the pool. What's Willa so worried about? The girl's old enough to go out by herself nights."

"Old enough. But kind of wild, too. Valerie's been in trouble before."

"What kind?"

"The State Police have arrested her twice for drunk driving. And last year the Fort Lauderdale police found her in a motel cabin with a man they arrested for a string of hold-ups."

Serena gave me another sidelong look. "Why are you interested in Valerie?"

I grinned at her. "She's sexy."

Serena drove the rest of the way in icy silence.

Carol Branco's motel made the Seaview look like a dump. It was a great deal larger, with five separate wings fanning out to the beach from a central building that held the lobby, two restaurants, a cocktail lounge and a smallish nightclub. It was gleaming white, set among lush tropical vegetation like a combination of the Taj Mahal and a Mediterranean palace. It had more palms, more private beach, more swimming pool, more Cadillacs and foreign sports cars, more fat people of both sexes too rich to give a damn what they looked like in their gaudy sports clothes, more sleek ones of both sexes wearing minute swim suits to show what the rich ones were paying for.

I left my car in one of the parking areas and found the room whose number Serena had given me as belonging to Carol Branco. It was in a small wing fronting the beach, utterly hidden from curious eyes by olive trees and massive groupings of frangipani and hibiscus. Which came in handy when my knock at her door drew no response. I got a stiff strip of plastic from my pocket and used it to spring the lock open, went inside and quickly shut the door behind me.

Her room wasn't big enough to get lost in, but it was big enough. There was a pink-and-blue sleeping area, and a separate area furnished as a luxurious sitting room. The bathroom was all marble tile, with an oversized sunken bathtub. I went through the place quickly the first time, hunting for some insight into the problem of Carol Branco. She smoked a great deal, most of her clothes were expensive and brandnew, and those with store labels came from Miami and Miami Beach. So not only didn't she have a TV contract in New York—she hadn't been living in New York.

That was a bit of background on her, but not much. It didn't tell me why Lou Kovac had become interested in her. I stood looking at the closed door for a few moments, considering how delighted acting Police Chief Hollis Cobb would be at the opportunity to lock me up for breaking-and-entering with intent to commit burglary. Then I decided to hell with it. I was fed up with moving around in the dark. I began a professional search of the place.

The drawers, her luggage, a spare handbag in one of the closets and an opera bag in the vanity contained no personal papers at all. No letters, no identification, no notes to herself; no shopping list, theater stub or address book. Which was unusual in itself. I pulled out drawers and looked behind them and under them, checked luggage and handbag for hidden compartments, rummaged through the wastebaskets. There had to be something. But there wasn't.

That made me stubborn. I looked under the bed mattress, the cushions of the sofa and chairs, turned the chairs over and examined their bottoms, flipped over the rugs, peered under the bathroom sink, inspected the backs of the pictures on the walls.

It was behind a round, framed mirror that hung next to Carol Branco's bed: A hole about the size of a quarter had been cut through the wall.

I took the mirror off its hook and laid it on the bed. I put my eye to the hole in the wall but couldn't see anything. The canvas back of a framed painting blocked the view on the other side of the wall. Poking my pen through the hole, I moved the painting aside enough to peek into the other room. It was smaller than Carol Branco's, furnished in stark modern. No one appeared to be in it at the moment.

Taking up the mirror again, I inspected the back of it. The brown paper covering its back hung loose from a single tack at the top. I raised the paper, and found myself looking through the back of the mirror at the bed.

A two-way job—an ordinary mirror if looked at from the front, a clear round window if looked at from the back.

I put the two-way mirror down, left Carol Branco's room, and went along the shrubbery-curtained walk to the room next to it. The number on the door was 46. I knocked and waited a moment, to be sure. Then I used the strip of plastic to get inside.

The room was uninhabited. There was no luggage, no clothing in the closets or drawers, not even anything left behind in the wastebaskets. The framed picture I'd jiggled with my fountain pen hung crooked on the wall between that room and Carol Branco's. It was a Degas print. I pushed it aside and put my eye to the hole in the wall, found myself looking through the wall at Carol Branco's bed and the area around it.

Straightening the picture to hide the hole, I went back to the other room and hung the two-way mirror back in place. Then I went back to my Olds, got my hip flask from the glove compartment, and carried it into the motel lobby.

Managing a faintly embarrassed manner for one of the room clerks, I told him my problem. "I threw a party at my place the other day. One of the crowd left this behind." I showed him the flask. "Trouble is, I don't remember his name or which of my friends brought him. All I remember is, he told me he was staying here, in number 46. I just went down and knocked at his room, but nobody answers."

It was crude, but the clerk had no reason to be suspicious so it got me what I wanted.

"Forty-six . . ." the clerk said, thinking. "Oh, yes—Mr. Martin Roy."

"Sounds like that could be the name. What's he look like?"

"Tall. About your height. But thin. With brown hair. He wears glasses."

I nodded. "That's him."

"But he checked out this morning."

I made a face. "Dammit, I'd like to send this on to him. Probably doesn't remember where he left it. He was pretty swacked. Did he leave a forwarding address?"

He hadn't. But the clerk got out Martin Roy's card for me. It had the home address he'd given when signing in. A Miami address. It could have been phony. So could his name. But he'd arrived in his own car, and as a matter of course his license number had been noted on the record card. A Florida plate. I copied Martin Roy's name and address on a scrap of paper—and the license number. While at it I noted that Roy had registered at the motel almost three weeks ago.

I thanked the clerk, went back to my car, and headed for the home of Carol Branco's mother.

The street had trees and high hedges, like the street on which the Fergusons lived. But there the resemblance ended. These trees were old and discouraged, like the neighborhood. The tall hedges were wild, untended. The houses behind them were small frame and stucco structures in need of a bath and a fresh coat of paint. I parked in front of the address Serena had given me.

Hedge branches tilted across the path opening. I pushed through and saw that the hedge went all the way around Mrs. Branco's property, cutting off any view of the neighboring houses. The house itself was a one-story cottage in the middle of what had once been a lawn but was now sun-withered grass and weeds and bare spots. It had a flimsy porch with a weather-beaten, sagging sofa on it—and a brand-new rocking chair. I went up onto the porch and rang the bell. It made a loud, unmusical sound inside, but it didn't bring anybody to the door.

I rang again and it got me the same. Going off the porch, I walked around the house. The shades were all down to keep out the sun. A bare wire ran from a hook on the rear wall to a branch of a mangy lemon tree. Hanging from the wire by clothespins were an apron, a flowered dress, a slip and three pairs of woman's socks. They belonged to a small woman. They were dry, but with the hot sun all that told me was that they hadn't been hung out within the past fifteen minutes.

There was another opening in the wild hedge back there. I looked through it. A dirt path meandered between other people's hedges toward both ends of the block. I went to

Mrs. Branco's back door, opened the screen and knocked. Nothing.

I hesitated, glancing at my watch. I had an hour to go till six o'clock, nothing special to do with that hour, and a large amount of frustrated curiosity building up in me. It seemed to be my day for breaking and entering.

Any burglar will tell you about people who, before they go out, lock the front door and all the windows—and forget about the back door. I tried the knob. Mrs. Branco was apparently one of those people. The door wasn't locked. I went in and closed the door behind me.

With the shades down, it was dim inside, making me squint to see things clearly. I was in a large kitchen that also served as a dining room. In contrast to the outside of the house, the interior was orderly and clean. A cup, saucer, bread plate, coffee pot and pint milk bottle had been washed and set on the drainboard beside the sink to dry. They were dry. A dish towel hung neatly over one of the chairs around a square table covered with a checked oilcloth that had been wiped spotless. I went through the kitchen to the rest of the small house.

There was a short, murky hallway. A small bathroom, its tiles cracked but shining with cleanliness. Several closet doors. A half-open door led me into the final room of the cottage.

The closed shades filled the room with gloomy half-light. Judging by the old, dark pieces of furniture, it was a bedroom by night, a living room by day. There was a large studio couch against one wall next to a bureau. Its back cushions and brown spread were scattered on the worn rug beside it. Its top sheet hung tangled over the side and the bottom sheet was very rumpled. It was odd for a woman who'd washed her breakfast dishes and tidied the rest of the place up to go out leaving her bed like that.

I was getting a strange, crawly feeling in my nerve endings. It might have been from going through too many doors without being invited. I moved deeper into the room, looking at the only two items that were new in the room. They were on a table beside an ancient wing chair: a copper lamp with ivy growing out of soil in its base; and beside it a silver-framed portrait photograph of a beautiful blonde woman.

She might have been thirty when the picture was taken. Or five years more or less. She had one of those faces that don't show age—its bones strong and finely molded, the skin firm. Her eyes were set far apart and slightly slanted. The nose had a nice tilt to it. Her mouth was exquisitely formed, a bit too small for my taste.

The crawly sensation was getting stronger. It made me wonder if I'd heard something out on the porch. I held myself still, listening.

Someone breathed behind me.

I didn't make the turn fast enough. A blanket came down over my head and face, enveloping me in musty darkness. A pair of arms wrapped themselves around me, imprisoning me in the blanket and pinning my arms to my sides. Their pressure sent pain flashing through my wounded arm, nearly immobilizing it. I twisted and shoved backward, off-balance and unable to break loose. The blanket flattened my nose and mouth, shutting off my air. The wool taste of it was against my tongue. My head wound and its effects weakened my struggle to get free, which in turn increased the effects of the wound. It got instantly worse when something hard struck me in the temple.

The blow wasn't hard enough to knock me all the way out. But it was enough to make my knees go loose and my brain spin dizzily. I yanked myself forward and to one side, gasping for breath and heard someone else panting through the blanket enshrouding me. I kicked out viciously The tip of my shoe connected with a shin. The shin jerked away and there was a stifled cry of pain. A woman's sound.

The arms continued to grip me like a vise; a man's arms, powerful as a blacksmith's. So there were two of them.

I kicked backward with my heel. He knew that game. His legs weren't there, and before I could try again he kicked me in the ankle and rammed both knees into the backs of mine. I fell down on my knees with his weight hanging on me. His arms didn't loosen. They dug my elbows into my sides. I finally managed to move my right hand enough to grip the Luger in my belt holster. But I couldn't draw it out. I tore at the blanket with my teeth, trying to bite a hole through it so I could breathe. A hard, cruel object came down against the top of my skull. Agony exploded downward to my shoulders, drenching me in sweat.

The fingers of my left hand found somebody's cloth-covered flesh and clamped as tightly as they could, twisting and pinching. The man holding me gasped and his arms loosened a bit. I twisted inside them, fighting to get the Luger out. The folds of the blanket fell away from my face for a moment and I was looking down at a man's brown suede shoe. The vise of his arms tightened again, blanketing my eyes. I had the Luger part way out of the holster by then. But part way wasn't enough. I used the last strength left to me to bend forward and force my head down in an attempt to bite his ankle.

I misjudged. My teeth closed through the blanket on his shoe. It would have to do. I bit down as hard as I could. My teeth tore through the blanket at last. I tasted suede and bit harder, trying to hurt the foot inside the shoe. He let out another gasp.

Then a hard object whiplashed the back of my ear and finished me.

Chapter 9

THERE WAS THIS WOMAN. SHE STOOD AND LOOKED DOWN at me. I lay on my back on the floor and looked up at her.

She was a small woman, though from my position her head seemed to be touching the ceiling. It was the same ceiling. The same room. Mrs. Branco's living room. The woman wore a bargain basement dress that hung loosely on her too-thin frame. She was in her fifties, with gray-streaked yellow hair and a work-worn face that bore some resemblance to the blonde in the silver-framed portrait. Her face had deep, harsh lines in it, but was not unkindly. Just cautious and puzzled.

My face was wet and drops of water ran slowly over my ears and throat. She held an empty glass in her hand. I blinked up at her and made a sound in my throat.

"Who are you?" she snapped. "What are you doing in my house? What happened to you?"

I assigned myself a work-project: get up off the floor. I rolled over and got my elbows under me, and that was all I could manage for the moment. Rest period. My left arm was numb. My head was a sore, swollen lump. I touched the bandage on my forehead, felt a wet spot. The bullet crease had opened and bled a little. But I was alive, and I hadn't expected to be.

Somebody had shot at me and planted dynamite in my car. That somebody wanted me very dead. I'd assumed it was the same somebody who'd ambushed me in Mrs. Branco's house. Obviously I'd been wrong. So who had ambushed me? Also, why?

I picked up my head and looked at the small woman's bony shins. Neither bore a bruise mark. One of them would have, if I'd kicked it. She'd said "my house." That made her Carol Branco's mother.

The studio couch was ahead of me. It had been fixed up since I'd last seen it. The brown spread covered it without a crease. The cushions were neatly in place, leaning against the wall.

I got my knees under me and raised myself like a weight-lifter doing a five-hundred-pound press. I made it to the studio couch and sat down heavily, burying my face in my hands and breathing hard.

"What are you doing here?" Mrs. Branco demanded, more sharply this time.

It didn't sound like she'd called the cops yet. She seemed uncertain about me. I didn't want cops. Not the Coffin City variety, itching for an excuse to toss me in the clink. I spread my fingers and looked at her through them.

"You left your back door open," I croaked. "Shouldn't do that."

"I didn't," she stated firmly. "I never do. Not in this neighborhood."

"It was open anyway. So . . ."

"You're lying." Suspicion was gaining the upper hand in her. She wasn't afraid of me, though. She had no reason to be, if I looked the way I felt. I couldn't have held my own against Donald Duck. "You broke in here to rob my house."

"You have something here worth stealing?"

"No. But you wouldn't know that. . . . I'm afraid I'd better call the police."

"Wait . . ." I pleaded. "If I came in here to steal things, what was I doing on the floor? Taking a nap in the middle of the job?"

She thought that over. "Then what *are* you doing in my house?"

"The back door was partly open," I lied, "so I naturally figured you were home. When you didn't answer my knock, I stepped in and called for you. That was when somebody grabbed me from behind and slugged me."

"You mean somebody *else* came in here to rob me?" she said slowly, considering the possibility. "And you came and interrupted him?"

"Apparently."

She glanced around the room, saw nothing missing, stared at me again. "But how could he get in? I locked both doors before I left this morning. I know I did."

"Anybody else have a key to your house?"

"Just my daughter, while she's staying in town."

I'd kicked a woman's shin. It had unquestionably been a woman's cry of pain. I said, "Then he must have opened the door some other way. Burglars have ways, I hear."

She still wasn't convinced. "But who are you? Why did you come here?"

"I'm a reporter. From Miami. I wanted to interview you about your daughter's career in television."

"But why'd you come here? I'm never home during the day. I work."

"I didn't know that." I let go of my face and fished two of those wonderful little white pills out of my pocket. "Could I please have some water?"

She looked at the pills. "What are those?"

"Codeine. And I need them right now."

"How come you carry them around with you?"

"I've been having chronic headaches lately," I told her dryly.

"Oh—migraines. I know how that is. I have 'em myself." The last of her suspicion vanished. I'd established a bond between us. Fellow sufferers. "Only codeine doesn't work with me any more. I have to go to bed and just ride it out. Wait and I'll bring you the water.''

She went out and came back with the glass refilled. I used all of it to wash down the pills and leaned back, resting my poor head on a cushion. My eyes began to close.

"That's a good idea," Mrs. Branco said soothingly. "Give the dope a chance to work."

I opened my eyes, but not much. There was something nagging at the back of my mind. Something I had to do. But I was too sick to find out what it was.

"Now I'd better call the police," she said.

"Why?"

"Well—about that man who broke in here. If he did try to rob me . . ."

"Nothing's missing, is it?"

"No, but . . ."

"And I didn't get a look at him. I couldn't describe him to the police. So what good would it do? They couldn't catch him without a description. And you can be sure he won't come back."

"I suppose not," she murmured. "After the scare you gave him."

"Yes. I scared him away, all right. So all you'd be able to do is make trouble for yourself."

"Well . . ." she said, giving in. "If you really think I shouldn't . . ."

"I do," I said. "I really do." I let my eyes close.

When I opened them again, Mrs. Branco was sitting in a chair with her hands resting on her bony knees, watching over me like a shop-worn angel.

"How long was I out?" I asked sleepily.

"About half an hour." She smiled at me. "Feel better now, don't you?"

I did feel better. I also remembered what it was that I'd had to do. I sat up and looked at my watch. Quarter-to-seven. Three-quarters of an hour past time.

"I've been wondering," Mrs. Branco said. "What's that bandage on your forehead for? Were you in an accident?"

"Uh-huh. Auto collision. Can I use your phone, Mrs. Branco?"

There were limits to her kindness. Even with a fellow sufferer. "Long distance to Miami?"

"No. A local call."

"Oh." Her face softened again. "Sure you can."

The phone was on top of the bureau. She got it down for me. I set it on my lap and dialed the Seaview Motel. The night clerk answered. I said who I was and asked if there had been any calls for me.

"Yeah," he told me. "Some woman called. Wouldn't leave her name."

"When did she call?"

"Just a sec. I wrote it on a phone slip. . . . Oh, yeah, here it is. Six o'clock p.m. She called at six on the dot."

"Did she leave any message for me?"

"Nope. Sounded kinda upset you weren't in, but no message. I asked her. She said no."

"She didn't say she'd call back?"

"Uh-huh. Sorry."

I hung up, cursing under my breath. I was fairly sure the call had been bait to pull me into a trap. But, expecting it, I'd have had a chance to spring the trap without getting caught by it. Which might have gotten my hands on somebody with answers. Now I'd missed the chance. They'd try a different way next time, figuring I wasn't willing to risk returning to the Seaview Motel.

Mrs. Branco looked sympathetic. "Did you have a date?"

"Uh-huh."

"And she didn't wait? That's too bad. But maybe it's for the best. I don't think you're in any condition for a date tonight."

She was wrong about the kind of date I'd had. But she might have been right about the rest. The codeine had my headache under control, but the rest of me wasn't exactly perky.

"Like something to eat?" she suggested. "You wanted to talk about Carol. We could talk while we eat."

"I don't think I'm up to a meal right now."

"Just sandwiches and coffee. Do you good."

She went off to the kitchen. When she came back it was with the snack meal on a tray. I managed half a ham sandwich and two cups of black coffee. The coffee helped. I told her my editor in Miami had read the story about her daughter in the *Clarion* and decided it was a good human interest piece for our paper—since it was in Miami that she'd won the beauty contest that started her on her road to fame. I felt unpleasant doing it. But that's what I told her.

She glowed with parental pride. "A lot of people around here didn't think Carol was going to make out well when she decided to go off and seek her fortune. Now they know how wrong they were. I could have told them. A girl as lovely as Carol . . ." She looked toward the silver-framed portrait on the table. "That's her. She gave me that, when she came back. Isn't she lovely?"

"Very. At least in that picture. I haven't met her yet. I went to her motel, but she wasn't there."

"You'll probably find her in later. She likes to go off to the less crowded beaches during the day. If she phones me, I'll tell her about you, so she'll be certain to hurry back to her motel to meet you. She generally comes to see me or phones almost every day."

"Must be nice, having her back for a while."

"It sure is. Seeing her again, after ten years. It's not like I got other kids to keep me from being lonely. Carol's my only one. Branco and me got married kinda late in life for the kind've big family I'd've liked."

"She hasn't visited you since she went away? Ten years?"

"No." Mrs. Branco added defensively, "She was awfully taken up making a career for herself, you know. It ain't easy, for a girl out in the world alone. But sometimes she sent me postcards.''

"From California and New York?''

Mrs. Branco thought for a while. "I think so. And other places. Miami. Boston. Las Vegas. And once from Havana, Cuba. Carol tells me she had to move around a lot, on modeling assignments, till she began to get breaks on TV. I didn't even know about that till she came back here all successful and everything. It was quite a surprise, I can tell you. A wonderful surprise. How come you ain't taking any notes for your newspaper story?''

"I've an excellent memory. Never take notes.'' We talked about her daughter's career. What she told me tallied with the story Carol Branco had given Serena. I watched Mrs. Branco carefully, and became certain that she believed her daughter's version of her past ten years. That Carol had won a beauty contest in Miami seemed to be a fact. Her daughter had sent newspaper clippings about it. After that there'd been the postcards from her daughter, with vague references to modeling jobs. Then the big surprise when Carol returned home looking successful and giving out the story that she was going to be a television star.

"Your daughter has never married?'' I asked her.

"No. Not that she hasn't had offers, a beautiful girl like Carol. She was telling me about some of the real big men that've asked her to marry them, in Hollywood and New York. A movie actor, a TV producer—men like that. But she's turned 'em all down. Not that she ain't normal. Carol likes men, always did. But she wants to be a success as an actress first. Prove herself on her own. It was the same back here, before she went away. All the boys were crazy about her. And there was this was one nice boy she almost did marry. But then she changed her mind and went off to try to become a movie star. That's what she wanted, even back then. She knew she was beautiful; she was sure she'd make it if she only tried. Of course I was against it. Turns out now she knew what she was doing, but I couldn't know that at the time. We even fought about it. I wanted her to marry him and settle down. He was such a nice, clean-cut boy from a good family. I always did like Gil.''

"Gil." I said it woodenly.

Mrs. Branco nodded. "Gil Hurley. He's a successful lawyer now. And running for Chief of Police."

Chapter 10

"THEY WENT STEADY THEIR LAST YEAR IN HIGH SCHOOL," Mrs. Branco told me. "But after they graduated, Carol broke off with him. All the boys were after her. She said she'd decided she was too young to settle down to just one yet. So Gil went off to college. But then after a couple years he came back here for summer vacation and they started going steady again. Gil was so much in love with her, and so afraid of losing her, he even quit college. Got a job in the bank here, as a teller, just so he could stay around her."

"What happened to break them up?"

Mrs. Branco shrugged. "Nothing special. They went together about two years. Gil wanting to marry her, and Carol putting him off. You see, she always had this itch in the back of her mind—the notion she ought to go off and make something of herself. She always figured she had what it took to become something big. So finally she just made up her mind and went."

"How'd Hurley take it?"

"He was heartbroken. So was I. He used to drop around here, from time to time. We'd talk about how maybe she'd change her mind, after she'd been out in the cold world awhile, and come back. But she didn't. And when she won that beauty contest, Gil finally gave up. He went back to college and became a lawyer. He's married now. To the richest woman in the county. John Coffin's widow. That was a surprise. For a while there, everybody thought she was gonna marry Monte Ferguson.''

"Ferguson?'' I said stupidly. "She was going to marry him?''

"Well—neither of 'em ever said so. But Ferguson began to manage her real estate after Coffin died. They saw a lot of each other, and then they began going out together, evenings. And so naturally everybody figured . . . But then she started going places with Gil, instead. And it was him she married.''

"Has Hurley been around here since your daughter came back?''

"No. But Carol told me she saw him, right after she got back. He was making a campaign speech in the high-school auditorium, and she went to hear it. Went up and talked to him afterwards. She says Gil was real pleased to see her, and happy for her success.''

"Has she seen him since then?''

"Not that she's mentioned to me. Why?''

I shifted the subject. We talked some more about her daughter, but I didn't find out anything else I could use. Before I left, Mrs. Branco insisted on calling her daughter's motel on the chance that she'd be in. She wasn't.

I got Doctor Kerner's address from her and went there to get my bandages changed. The doctor didn't like the way my wounds had reopened. He accused me of not taking care of myself. I agreed with him.

It was dark when I drove into the Coffin estate. The Cuban houseboy carried my suitcase into the guest house. He told me that Gil and Willa Hurley had gone off to some campaign meeting together, but would be back in an hour or so. I hoped it wouldn't turn out to be longer. I wanted to talk to them, and I had very little steam left. My need for a solid night of healing sleep was making itself felt in no uncertain terms.

My accommodations were luxurious—a bedroom and sitting room in Danish modern, and an enormous bathroom with its very own fireplace. From the bedroom I could see the building housing the garage and servants' quarters. With the windows open, I'd be certain to hear when the Hurleys returned. If I was still conscious by then. I stripped and washed all over with cold water, regretting the bandages that prevented me from taking an icy shower. It helped, but not enough. I thought about the flask of brandy in my car. Getting into dark blue socks, slacks and polo shirt, I laced on a pair of black tennis sneakers and went out to the garage.

I took the Luger with me. Coffin City was too much of a shock to my nervous system. Events had proved that there was no place in or around it where I could relax with any feeling of safety. The next shock I got, someone else was going to get shocked back.

Leaving the garage with the flask in my left hand and the Luger in my right, I looked at my lighted windows in the guest house. I continued to watch them as I made my way back. Halfway there, a shadow flitted across the back wall of my sitting room.

I stood where I was, waiting. Whoever belonged to the shadow didn't show himself. I moved forward again, toward the lighted windows instead of the door. Crouching, I pushed through the flower bed lining the wall until I was under one of the open sitting-room windows. Holding my breath, I straightened, hooked a leg over the sill, and went in with the Luger, searching for someone to shoot.

The only someone in there was Willa's stepdaughter, Valerie. And she didn't look dangerous. Just a little drunk.

She sat on the couch drinking from a tall glass. On the low table in front of her was a tray with a bottle of scotch, a small ice bucket and an extra glass. She wore a pink satin robe that molded her upper body tightly, straining over the jutting cones of her breasts. It was held together in front by two big buttons. From her hips it flowed down in loose folds, covering her legs to her black-slippered feet. She wore dark eye make-up to go with her hair, but no lipstick, giving her mouth a naked look.

She gave me and my gun a startled stare. Then she grinned and stood up, raising her hands shoulderhigh, palms toward me.

"Don't shoot. I haven't any money on me, but you're welcome to what I do have."

She was more than a little drunk.

I put the Luger down, sat on one of the chairs, and poured brandy from the flask into the extra glass. I gulped it and leaned back wearily. "Don't you usually wait for an invitation?"

She was still standing with her hands up, grinning at me like a greedy cat watching a mouse. "I scared you, didn't I?"

"I scare easy."

She wrinkled her nose at me. "No, you don't. Private eyes are tough."

"Not this one. Not tonight. Who told you about me? Hugh Tallant?"

"Uh-huh."

"That where you went when you scooted out of here this afternoon?"

Valerie nodded, swaying a little. "After seeing you at the Algiers last night, I wondered what you were doing here, supposed to be a friend of Monte's."

"And Tallant told you. What else did he tell you about me?"

"That he was disappointed in you. He thought you'd be back in Miami by now."

"Where'd you go after you left Tallant?"

She shrugged. "Out on a yacht. Some boys were throwing a party. It was dull. They're that kind of boys."

"When'd you get back here?"

"Oh—about an hour ago. Why the third degree?"

I said, "Let's see your legs."

The tip of her tongue crept between her small, even teeth and fondled her lips. "You don't waste time."

"Your legs," I repeated. "Just up to your knees."

All she had to do was to raise the skirt of her robe. She didn't do that. What she did was to undo the two big buttons, grasp the front of her robe with both hands, and open it wide.

She wore black bikini panties that tilted across her slim, slinky hips at a rakish angle, showing her navel. That was all she had on under the robe. Her breasts were high, firm and full, snowy in contrast to the tan tinting the rest of her skin. Their pink tips were sharply pointed.

She didn't have a kick-bruise on either shin.

"Okay," I snapped. "You can cover up now."

"Why?" She let go of the front of her robe, but didn't close it.

I concentrated on pouring more brandy into the glass. "Seeing me here this afternoon upset you considerably, didn't it?"

"I was scared you'd tell—about me being with Hugh Tallant. How come you didn't?"

"I didn't want you sore at me."

"Maybe you hoped I'd be grateful to you?"

"Uh-huh. Something like that."

"I am grateful," Valerie purred. "Very." She bent toward me, her robe swinging wide open again. She put her hands on the arms of my chair on either side of me, and kissed me on the mouth. The silken waves of her raven's wing hair tickled my ears. Young as she was and liquored up as she was, she still packed voltage. Her mouth unglued itself from mine and the tip of her tongue flicked casually across my lips. Then she straightened slowly, the warm softness of her breasts caressing my face on the way up.

I poked the tip of a stiff forefinger into her belly button. It drove her backward, and she tripped and sat down hard on the couch.

"What the hell. . . ?"

"That's not the kind of grateful I meant," I told her. "It's information I want. Rein in your libido. No wonder everybody's worried about you getting into trouble."

"They call it trouble. I call it fun. What's the matter with you, Rome? Don't you like girls?"

"Not tonight, Josephine. It's been a big day. I'm a tired man."

She made a last try, but her heart wasn't in it any more. "You don't look *that* tired."

"I am, though. Old and tired. And in need of nourishing information. What's between you and Tallant?"

Instead of answering, she picked up her glass and drank the scotch in it. I let her drink all of it. Liquor oils the vocal cords.

When she put the glass down empty, I asked, "What would happen if I told your stepmother about you and Tallant?"

It scared hell out of her. "You wouldn't! My God, I don't come into my own money for another two years. She could cut off my allowance and make me go back to that lousy girls' school in Massachusetts. That rotten Gil Hurley's been trying to persuade Willa to do it anyway. He's so scared I'll get in some jam that'll hurt his election chances."

"What's so bad about the school in Massachusetts?"

"You don't *know*. They watch you like hawks. Dullsville."

"And around here it's funsville?"

"Sometimes."

"Especially with Hugh Tallant?"

Valerie made a face. "It has to be with him. He's all I get, lately. Ever since he took a notion to me, the kind of men I go for won't come near me. They're all afraid of Hugh. But Hugh's not so bad. At least he lets me play the wheel all I want."

"Lost much?"

She tried to be cagey, but she was too far gone to pull it off. "Some."

"More than your allowance," I hazarded.

"Hugh lets me gamble on credit. He's willing to trust me till I come into my money."

"I'll bet he is. You're a handy type of playmate for Tallant. Do you keep him filled in on all of Hurley's campaign plans?"

"That's not what Hugh wants me for," Valerie snapped.

"No. But it's a nice little extra. You do tell him what goes on around here, don't you?"

"I don't know anything to tell him. Nobody around here ever tells me what's going on. They're afraid I'll get tanked and spill it."

"But you overhear things from time to time. You couldn't help it. Did you tell Tallant about Lou Kovac?"

"I never even heard of him till Hugh told me about him today, when he was telling me what you are."

I let it go for the moment. "How well do you know Carol Branco?"

Valerie looked puzzled. "Who?"

"Carol Branco."

"Never heard of her."

"Come off it. There was a big story about her in the *Clarion* a couple weeks back."

"I never read Serena's hick paper."

Any further questions were interrupted by the sound of a car coming along the driveway toward the garage. Valerie glanced out the windows. A black Buick cruised into view, its headlights stabbing the darkness outside.

Valerie jumped to her feet, terrified. "Christ! If they catch me in here like this . . ." She clutched the front of her robe shut and got out of my rooms on the run, staggering slightly.

I finished my drink. The brandy did what it could for me. What I needed was a transfusion from somebody too young to know the meaning of tired blood.

Willa and Gil Hurley were coming along the path from the garage. I washed out Valerie's glass and brought it back with another glass I found in the bathroom. As I set them on the tray the Hurleys knocked at my door. I opened it and said hello and come in.

There was an interesting bulge in the right-hand pocket of his suit jacket. I managed to brush my hand over it as I ushered them in. It was a small revolver. I remembered Serena saying that Hurley had a .32 like hers.

Willa introduced me to her husband. He was staring as though I were the materialization of somebody he'd once met in a dream. He switched quickly to a professional smile and shook my hand. His grip was powerful, reminding me he'd played football in school. He hadn't softened any with the years. And he was a handsome lad, with a boyishness that was probably what got the ladies. I glanced at his shoes. They were black leather. I postponed asking if he had a pair of brown suede ones, not being up to coping with what might come of that.

"Like a drink?" I suggested. "I raided your liquor. Hope you don't mind."

They didn't mind. "I can use a drink," Willa said as she lowered herself to the couch. "These campaign meetings are so damn boring. Everybody saying the same things over and over again."

Gil Hurley sat beside her. "Better get used to them, honey. If things work out, we'll be attending a lot of them in the years to come."

I sat in the chair, facing them. "I understand you plan to use cleaning up Coffin City as a springboard to bigger things."

He gave me the grin of a man who is easily liked and knows it. I hadn't said or done anything to disturb him, and he'd decided I wasn't going to be trouble, after all. "That's the general idea, Tony."

"Police Chief to Governor of the state?"

"It can be done, with the proper backing. By the right man." The intensity of his ambition was showing. He softened it by adding, "I suppose that sounds conceited. Perhaps

I've been making too many campaign speeches. But if I don't believe in myself, I can't expect the voters to believe in me, can I?''

"Scotch or brandy?'' I said.

They wanted scotch on the rocks. I poured, dumped in the ice cubes, and poured myself another brandy injection. We sipped and I asked Hurley about Lou Kovac. He claimed to know nothing that the others hadn't told me. Kovac hadn't confided in him, had dealt mostly with Peck, his campaign manager, and Serena Ferguson. If Kovac had gotten onto something that hurt Tallant, Hurley said, he didn't know what it could be. And he had no idea why Kovac had returned to Miami. He met my eyes with open frankness as he answered my questions.

"I told Gil about Carol Branco,'' Willa said. "He can't understand why Kovac was interested in her, either.''

I watched Gil Hurley. "Any idea why she's lying about becoming a television star?''

"Haven't the foggiest notion,'' he said, a bit thickly. "Maybe Willa's theory is right. That Carol just wanted to make an impression on the old home town. Something like that.''

Willa asked, "Why don't you ask Carol herself about it?''

"I haven't been able to get in touch with her yet.'' I kept my eyes on Hurley. "You knew Carol Branco pretty well, didn't you?''

"I went to high school with her. Same as Willa.''

"I understand it went deeper than that. Weren't you and she planning to get married at one time?''

Willa replied for him: "They were very young. It was just kids' stuff. Fortunately, they both realized that in time.''

"Seen her since she came back?'' I asked Hurley.

He masked the shifting of his eyes by picking up his glass and drinking from it. "She came up to see me once, after I made a speech at the high-school auditorium. She wanted to wish me luck.''

"How about since then?"

Willa was watching him with narrowed, speculative eyes.

Hurley had more of his drink. "No, I only saw Carol that once. This campaign's been keeping me pretty busy." He shifted uncomfortably, aware of his wife's gaze upon him. "I don't see what connection this has with the work Kovac was doing for us."

"There has to be one," I pointed out. "Lou Kovac phoned New York to check on her, remember."

"Maybe he just found out she was lying about her career, and got curious."

I rolled the glass between my palms. "There's more to it than that. I had a look around Carol Branco's motel room this afternoon. There's a two-way mirror hanging on her wall. And behind it there's a peep-hole through the wall to the next room. The man who was using the next room checked in about the same time she did. Checked out this morning. I guess he got what he was after."

It seemed to bewilder them.

"You mean," Willa said, "that this man in the next room was a peeping tom? He made a hole in the wall so he could watch her . . . get undressed, and so forth?"

"No, a two-way mirror is a gimmick blackmailers use, to take the kind of photographs people wouldn't want passed around. That hole's perfectly placed to shoot pictures of Carol Branco's bed. And whoever happened to be on it."

Willa continued to look puzzled. I glanced at Gil Hurley. He was a pretty good actor, but something was ticking away inside him. Like a suddenly discovered time bomb.

"Perhaps," Willa ventured finally, "this blackmailer believes Carol's story about becoming a television star. Perhaps he feels she'll pay later to keep him from ruining her career. I'm sure she's had men in her room at night. She wouldn't have changed that much."

She said that last part maliciously, looking at her husband. He didn't say anything.

I shifted to a discussion of Hugh Tallant's most vulnerable spots—the spots into which Lou Kovac might have been digging. Hurley's mind was elsewhere, but he did his best to seem interested. He recalled that Lou Kovac had mentioned that gambling in several of Tallant's places appeared to be rigged in favor of the house. If that could be proven, it would hurt Tallant plenty, turning even the people who liked open gambling against him. We talked about Tallant's moonshine operations and I concluded that Tallant couldn't be hurt there. Both the Federal and State cops had tried, without success.

Finally Willa stood up and said, "I'm going to bed. When my nerves are keyed up like this it takes me hours to fall asleep."

She looked at Hurley. He followed her obediently, moving like a man in a trance.

After they'd gone, I finished the brandy in my glass, and thought about all the things that required doing that night. I wanted to go find Carol Branco and grill her. I wanted to keep an all-night vigil on Hurley, Willa and Valerie. I wanted to have a talk with the State cops. I wanted to phone Art Santini in Miami and get him to check up on Carol Branco and Martin Roy, the man who'd used the room next to her.

But I wasn't going to do any of those things. I was going to sleep. Whatever needed doing would have to wait till morning, when I'd had enough rest to do them properly. Within thirty-some hours I'd been shot, slugged and half smothered. If I forced myself to stay awake any longer, I'd be stumbling all over myself.

Turning off the lights, I kicked off my sneakers and stretched out on the bed with the Luger beside me. Consoling myself with the fact that at least I was near enough to the garage to be awakened by the sound of anyone driving in or out, I shut my eyes.

I passed out quickly. No dreams. I slept the sleep of the just. Or the unjust, after a hard day's wickedness.

* * *

I awoke with the impression that I'd heard something. It was dark. My hand closed on the Luger and I lay very still. Whatever it was that I heard, I didn't hear it again. There was no sound other than the surf spending a restless night on the beach. I looked at my watch in the shaft of moonlight sifting through the open window. It was ten minutes after two a.m.

I got up and prowled my rooms silently. Nobody there. I put on my tennis shoes, slipped out through the window and circled the guest house. Nobody and nothing. I felt as alone as a ghost wandering through the night with nobody to haunt.

I went to the garage. All the cars were still there. None of their hoods were hot. The lights were off in the servant's quarters upstairs. I followed the path in the other direction, through the walled gardens and foliage-enclosed terraces toward the main house. I met no one on the way, and there were no lights showing there, either.

I returned to the guest house and went back to sleep.

Maybe it was a sense of guilt about sleeping the night away. When I woke again it was only six in the morning, and I couldn't force myself back into sleep. So I got up. I brushed my teeth, drank two glasses of cold water, used more of it on my face, and went out for a stroll.

No one else was up yet. The air was fresh and crisp. The sun sparkled brilliantly on the ocean without being hot. I wandered down toward the water.

There was a flagstone path along the edge of the estate's private stretch of beach. I followed it aimlessly. Beyond the main house the depth of the estate narrowed till I could get glimpses of the public road off to my right. I came to a small private dock. A narrow paved driveway led from it to the road. There was a twenty-foot outboard cruiser moored to the dock. It was a sleek job, designed to be driven at high speed by its two outboards. Boatmen have an instant interest in other people's boats. I strolled onto the dock for a closer look.

Gil Hurley lay on his back in the cockpit, his arms outflung, his legs sprawled, his sightless eyes staring up at the sky.

He'd been shot through the chest. The heart region. The blast had left scorch marks around the bloody bullet hole in his shirt.

Chapter 11

HE WAS STILL IN THE SAME CLOTHES HE'D BEEN WEARING the night before. There were long scratches down the left side of his face, the kind clawing fingernails could have made. His fingers were curled stiffly. I went down on one knee beside him and pried gently at the fingers of his right hand. They didn't give. There was a bruise across the knuckles. The hand was like cold marble. He'd been dead for hours.

His gun wasn't in his pocket. I looked around and didn't find it.

I straightened and got out a Lucky and lit it. I sat on the low cabin overhang and smoked and looked at Gil Hurley. The crew-cut looked indecent on a dead man. His mouth was open, showing his teeth, and his face was contorted by his last, brief agony. It wasn't a face that had been young and good-looking and ambitious. I looked in the direction of the buildings. They couldn't be seen from there. I snapped the burned-down stub of my cigarette into the water and walked back to the guest house.

Using the sitting room phone, I called the nearest State Police office and got Lieutenant Waine's home number. He answered his phone on the seventh ring, sounding half asleep. I told him who I was and that Lieutenant Santini had advised me to get in touch with him. By the time I finished filling him in on what I was doing in Coffin City, he was wide awake.

"I'd give up a week's vacation for something to hit that Tallant crowd with," Waine said. "Got anything for me?"

"What I've got is a murder." I told him about Gil Hurley.

Waine was silent for a few seconds. Then he asked quietly, "You called Hollis Cobb about this yet?"

"No. I thought I'd better let you know first."

"Leave it at that. Don't call him. I'll drop by on my way and tell him. And I'll bring our own medical examiner and a couple lab boys with me. Cobb can't very well refuse to let us come along. Coffin City doesn't have lab men of its own. He'd have to call us in on it eventually, anyway. This way we're right there with him, to make sure there isn't any messing around with evidence."

"Bring a diver along, too," I told him. "Hurley was shot at very close range by what looks to be a small-caliber bullet. And he's been carrying a .32 around with him since he started running for Police Chief. He had it on him last night. He doesn't now. It might be in the water, under the boat."

"Will do," Waine said. And then: "Quite a thing—the man running against Cobb getting himself knocked off just three weeks before election. Doesn't look good for the Tallant crowd, does it?" He didn't sound sad about it.

My next call was to Carol Branco's motel. She wasn't in. I told the room clerk that I was Lieutenant Waine of the State Police. "We've found a red Jaguar abandoned off the highway. It may be Miss Branco's. Was she in at all last night?"

"Yes, she was, Lieutenant," the clerk told me. "But she got a phone call around one o'clock this morning and went out."

"Driving the Jaguar?"

"Yes. Has something happened to her?"

"That's what I'm trying to find out. She hasn't come back yet?"

"No, she hasn't."

"Who phoned her at one a.m.?"

"I don't know. I took the call and just plugged it through

to her room. It was a man's voice that asked for her. That's all I can tell you."

"Do you have the license number of her car?"

"Yes—" He went away and came back a moment later, reading the number of her plate to me. It was a New York license.

I copied it down and said, "Looks like I've bothered you for nothing. The Jaguar we found has a different number."

"Oh." He sounded relieved. "I'm glad to hear that."

"Sure. Sorry to've bothered you." I hung up.

A man had phoned Carol Branco at one in the morning. She'd gone out. It was now going on seven and she hadn't come back. Gil Hurley was dead in the clothes he'd been wearing last night. Something had awakened me about two in the morning. Guesswork before breakfast is a futile business.

I headed for the servant's quarters over the garage. It turned out that the only servants who slept in were the Cuban houseboy and his plump, pretty wife, who worked as a maid. I woke them and asked if either of them had heard a shot during the night. The question frightened them. They swore they'd heard nothing. They both worked hard all day and slept hard all night. Waiting impatiently while they got dressed, I went to the main house with them.

The houseboy went to the kitchen to brew coffee. His wife took me upstairs, to the Hurleys' bedroom.

It was a large, sumptuous room, with a very wide canopy bed. Willa Hurley was asleep on one side of it, lying stiffly on her back with her arms straight down at her sides, breathing harshly through her teeth. The maid said her name sharply a couple times. Willa didn't stir.

Muttering something about sleeping pills, the maid shook Willa's shoulder. Willa's eyes unglued slowly. "Wha . . . what?" she asked in a thick, hoarse voice.

"Please get up, Mrs. Hurley," I said. "Something's happened. Get dressed and come downstairs. It's important."

She forced herself to a sitting position, looking at me groggily and running shaky fingers through her tangled hair. She wasn't faking. She'd definitely drugged herself to sleep. Whether she'd done so before or after the shooting was another question. The other half of the bed hadn't been slept in. The pillow there was smooth and fat, undented.

While Willa struggled to clear some of the fog from her brain, I prowled the room, opening the doors to the clothes closets. In one of them were Hurley's shoes—six pairs of them. One pair was brown suede. I examined those closely. On one of them were dent marks that could have been made by my teeth.

"What time is it?" Willa grated.

I put the shoes down. "Almost seven."

"What's the matter? What's happened?"

"I'll be waiting for you downstairs. Try not to take long." I went out of the room, taking the maid with me.

"Now the girl's room."

She took me down to the far end of a thick-carpeted corridor. Valerie's bedroom was smaller than Willa's and Hurley's, but equally sumptuous. And the bed was just as wide. Valerie was curled up on her side in the middle of it, stark naked.

The Cuban maid hurriedly got Valerie's robe off the back of a chair and draped it over her. She shook Valerie a couple of times. The girl growled without opening her eyes, and curled up tighter. There was a half-empty bottle of scotch on a television set next to her bed. People who drink themselves to sleep hate to wake up before they've slept it off. I pinched one of her bare toes, hard.

She sat up snarling, the robe sliding off her torso and bunching around her hips. The maid fled from the room.

"Get up and get dressed," I told her. "I'll wait for you downstairs."

"Go to hell!" she screeched, slurring the words. "What's the lousy . . ."

"And hurry it up," I said. "You don't want to be like this when the cops come."

"Cops?" That cleared her head a little. "What's going on?"

"You'll find out when you come down. Better make it fast."

I went down to the green and gold living room. The maid appeared almost instantly, carrying coffee and toast on a tray. She set it down and vanished again.

I finished one cup of black coffee and was on my second when Willa came down the stairs. She came slowly, grasping the bannister rail tightly. Her face was pale and bloated.

"What's happened?" she demanded weakly as she reached the bottom of the steps. "You'll have to forgive me for . . . I took some pills to help me sleep. They haven't worn off yet and . . . Where's Gil?"

I poured coffee into another cup. "Have some of this. You need it."

She stood staring at the cup I held out. Then she looked up at my face again. "Where's Gil?"

"Didn't he go to bed with you last night?"

"I was restless, couldn't sleep," she said vaguely, trying to concentrate. "We sat up for a couple hours together, watching television and having a couple more drinks." She frowned with the effort of remembering. "Finally I took some sleeping pills and when they started working I went to bed."

"What about your husband?"

"Not right away. He decided to stay up a bit longer, reading in the library."

"Did he go to bed at all last night?"

"I don't know . . ." Then she repeated it with rising hysteria: "I don't know! Why? Where's Gil? What's happened to him?"

Valerie was coming down the stairs, in tight toreador pants and a fluffy yellow sweater, looking cranky and hung-over.

I said, "Your husband's been shot, Mrs. Hurley. He's dead."

Valerie's mouth opened with shock. Then she almost grinned. Then she shut her mouth, narrowed her eyes, and made her face expressionless.

Willa stared at me blankly for several seconds. Then she sat down on the edge of the sofa behind her and began to shake. Valerie went over and sat beside her. She put her arm around her stepmother and murmured, "Take it easy, dear. . . . Easy does it." Her voice was surprisingly tender.

The door chimes sounded, and it was the cops.

It was another hour before I got around to having my toast and another cup of coffee. By then the law was out at the boat and Willa was back in her room. She had plenty of company—Valerie, Monte Ferguson and her doctor. I had company, too. Serena sat stiffly on the edge of the couch, twisting a handkerchief between her nervous hands. Her face showed strain and shock, nothing else. Seymour Peck paced up and down thoughtfully, looking a bit upset and more than a bit impatient.

Valerie had phoned them, and they'd rallied around swiftly. None of them had an explanation for what had happened. Ferguson, Peck and Serena had spent the entire previous night in blameless sleep, so they said. It seemed I was the only one whose night had been interrupted. Willa had heard no shot. Valerie had drunk herself to sleep by midnight and hadn't heard any shot either. It was possible.

Peck stopped pacing and said, to no one in particular, "This is going to necessitate some fast changes in our campaign plans."

Serena looked at him. "You mean now *you'll* be the reform candidate for Chief of Police."

Peck blinked at her. "I suppose that's right." He spoke as though it hadn't occurred to him till she said it.

"Just as you wanted it originally," Serena said bitterly. "Before Willa decided differently."

"Of course I wanted it," Peck chided Serena. "But not at the expense of Gil's death. You know I feel as badly about it as you do."

"Oh, sure. But you're already busy making plans."

Peck made a helpless gesture. "Somebody has to."

I drained my cup and refilled it. "Serena, what was your relationship with Gil Hurley?"

She frowned at me. "We were friends."

"Were you more than friends?"

"Of course not," she snapped, too quickly. "What do you mean?"

Peck answered for me. "Rome probably means before Gil married Willa. When you and Gil used to go together for a time."

Serena bit her lip and mashed the handkerchief into a tight wad between her palms. "Oh, that. . . . Yes, we did go out on dates for a while. Before Gil married Willa."

"And since then?"

"There's been nothing between Gil and me since then," Serena flared. "What are you insinuating?"

I sipped coffee and watched her, saying nothing. She blushed a little, under the tan, but she didn't look away.

"I was only wondering," I said finally.

"You have a very nasty mind."

I nodded. "Afraid so."

Monte Ferguson came down the stairs looking like he'd been through a wringer.

"Doctor Hale's given Willa a sedative injection," he told us wearily. "He didn't want to, on top of the sleeping pills she took last night, but it became necessary. She was so wild. We couldn't calm her down." He wiped a hand slowly over his face. "Kept repeating that she was all alone again. First Coffin died and left her alone. And now Gil."

"She's not exactly alone," I said mildly. "She's got you."

Ferguson wrinkled his forehead at me. "Yes, that's true. She does have her friends. . . . I could use some of that coffee."

He sat down and poured coffee in a cup. He drank some of it and shook his head as though it was hard to shake. "I still can't take it in. Gil murdered. Who could have done it?"

Peck let out a short, unpleasant laugh. "That's not hard to guess."

"You mean Hugh Tallant?" Ferguson looked to me. "Do you think so?"

Instead of answering, I said, "Tell me about Hurley and Carol Branco."

It didn't startle Ferguson. He asked me gravely, "Do you think she has something to do with what's happened?"

"Something. You should have spilled what you knew when you learned about Lou Kovac's interest in her."

"But I didn't know anything. It was just that . . . it made me wonder. About the possibility that Gil and Carol Branco had . . . taken up with each other again, since she came back."

Serena was staring at her brother. "Gil and Carol Branco?"

He nodded at her. "They were going to be married at one time. You were too young then to know about it. He was terribly broken up when she called it off and went away." Ferguson looked at me. "I don't like to say this, but . . . I don't think Gil ever felt about any other woman the way he did about her."

"You think when she came back, they took up where they'd left off?"

"If they did, I didn't know about it." Ferguson gazed into his cup. "It did occur to me as being possible, when you told me that Kovac had been checking on her."

"Did it occur to Willa Hurley, too?"

He didn't look up. "I don't know," he said flatly.

Hollis Cobb came through the pool patio doors, followed

by deputy Luke LaFrance and Lieutenant Waine of the State Police. Waine was professionally solemn, Cobb looked shaken, and it was the first time I'd seen LaFrance minus his joviality.

"Our man's still diving under the boat," Waine told me. "He still hasn't found Hurley's gun." He was a big, solid man with shrewd eyes in a rugged, weatherbeaten face. Looking around the room, he asked, "Where's Mrs. Hurley?"

"You can't talk to her now," Ferguson told him. "The doctor has given her something to put her to sleep. He said she mustn't be disturbed."

Hollis Cobb was gazing at me without affection. "What's the big idea calling the State cops? Whyn't you call me, first?"

I smiled at him, saying nothing.

"The answer to that is obvious," Peck told him nastily. "He knew you wouldn't be interested in finding Gil's murderer. But you needn't think Gil's death will help you win . . ."

"*Help* me?" Cobb snarled. "You think I'm stupid? I know damn well how it'll look to everybody. I know what it can do to my chances."

LaFrance leaned against a wall with his hands in his pockets, staring at nothing. "I still can't believe it," he muttered. "I looked at him in that boat, but I couldn't take it in that he was really dead."

I looked at him over my cup. "Made you feel bad, did it?"

His eyes focused on me. "Yeah," he said softly. "Surprised? Politics don't mean that much to me. I've known Gil all his life. He used to go out fishing with me, when he was a kid." LaFrance's voice took on a force that startled me: "If I get my hands on whoever did it . . ."

Lieutenant Waine looked at the rest of us. "Medical examiner says Hurley probably was killed somewhere between midnight and three this morning.''

"Something woke me up around two this morning," I told him. "That could have been it."

"It doesn't seem to have wakened anybody else around here," Waine said. "But we'll soon know. Luckily, we know when Hurley had his last meal, so the autopsy should be able to pinpoint the time of his death pretty exactly. Now—if any of you know anything about his murder . . .''

"If you don't mind, Lieutenant," Cobb grated, "I'll conduct this investigation. It's in my jurisdiction, remember."

Waine shrugged his heavy shoulders. "Just trying to help."

"Help when I ask for help." Cobb looked round. "Okay, I already got Rome's story. Where's Valerie Coffin?"

I got up and went out to the patio. Lieutenant Waine followed me. We walked along together, and then Waine said, "Any ideas?"

"Too many." We stopped at the edge of the swimming pool. "Seymour Peck is going to run for Chief of Police in Hurley's place. What're the reform party's chances of getting him elected?"

"Damn good, I'd say. The killing's bound to make a lot of the voters think hard thoughts about Tallant's gang. What Cobb said about this hurting him could be true."

"Uh-huh. Cobb's not dumb."

"No," Waine agreed. "Whatever Cobb is, he's not dumb. Used to be a top man with the vice squad up in Jacksonville, before they bounced him for grabbing more than his share of the graft, four years ago. Tallant hired him right away and brought him down here. He makes a perfect Chief of Police—for Tallant."

"What were the reform party's chances of beating him *before* Hurley's murder?"

"Not bad. Fifty-fifty, I'd say." Waine grew thoughtful. "Better, if I could nail Cobb for something before election."

"You referring to anything specific?"

"Maybe. . . . I got an anonymous phone call a week ago. Some guy who claimed Cobb's been seeing a lot of an under-age girl in another part of the county. He said he'd let me know the details the next time Cobb went to visit her. Could've been just a crank call, of course. But if I could catch Cobb red-handed with her . . ." The prospect pleased him.

"Impairing the morals of a minor?"

Waine nodded happily. "Maybe even statutory rape. Well—let's get back to the subject of Hurley."

I gave him what I had, a meager present. Mostly, I told him about Carol Branco—the things I knew to be facts, other things that seemed likely, and some that were pure guess-work.

He copied down the license number of her red Jaguar. "I'll send out a check on her. Not that we've got anything to book her on."

"Just try to find her," I said. "And to find out where she was last night. I'll call you later, from Miami."

"Why Miami?"

"Carol Branco's clothes are from Miami. The guy who had the room next to hers registered as being from Miami. Lou Kovac got it in Miami. That's why."

Waine walked me to the garage. I got the stick of dynamite out of the glove compartment and gave it to him.

Waine looked at it in his hand. "Nice friendly gesture."

"I didn't think so at the time."

I drove away from the Coffin estate and pulled into the first roadhouse I came to, to make some phone calls.

The first was to Mason, the New York private detective who'd checked on Carol Branco for Lou Kovac. I gave him the number of the New York license plate on Carol Branco's Jaguar, and asked him to check it out for me and phone the information to my office.

"It'll cost you," Mason said. "Cut rates to the trade, but it'll still cost. And you owe me for the last time I called you."

"Bill me. I'll send you a check."

"Another thing," Mason said hopefully. "Your pal Kovac never got around to paying for the job I did for him. Now maybe he won't be able to. I hate to bring it up—but business ain't exactly been thriving lately, and I got to eat and pay rent."

I said I knew how that could be, and that he could send me Lou Kovac's bill along with mine.

My next call was to Art Santini. He told me that Lou Kovac was gaining, but still not fit to talk, and that they still hadn't turned up the two hoods who'd worked Kovac over. I asked him to check out the license number of the car driven by Martin Roy, the man who'd had the room next to Carol Branco.

A call to Carol Branco's motel got me the information that she still hadn't returned, so I phoned her mother.

Mrs. Branco said she hadn't seen or heard from her daughter since I'd left her house. And she had no idea where she could be. "It must be very annoying for you, I know," she said sympathetically, "after you came all the way up here from Miami to interview Carol. I'm sorry you're having so much trouble getting together with her."

I said I was sorry about it, too.

Chapter 12

Lou Kovac had been moved to a small private room with his own nurse, and this time there was no fuss about admitting me, on my promise not to stay long. It wasn't a difficult promise to keep. A few minutes of standing by the bed looking down at his broken figure and sunken face was all I could take. The nurse told me that he hadn't been fully conscious, or said anything intelligible, in all the time she'd been tending him. All the visit got me was a re-sharpening of my fury. I still had no one to use its sharpness on.

I used a phone booth in the hospital waiting room to call Santini. His license check told me that the man in the motel room next to Carol Branco's hadn't expected what he'd been doing to bring him trouble. He'd registered under his right name: Martin Roy. A cross-check of his operator's license revealed that he was six feet tall, weighed a hundred and sixty pounds, had blue eyes and brown hair, and that his license was valid only when wearing corrective lenses. Which agreed with the room clerk's description of Martin Roy. Santini said he had no police record in Miami or Dade County. He gave me the address listed for him. It was the one he'd used when he'd registered at the motel. I drove to it.

It was in a cramped, overcrowded Miami neighborhood of narrow streets and seedy buildings and cracked, dirty sidewalks; of flea-bag hotels and Cuban bars and the empty, bitter faces of exiles—refugees from political upheavals, financial disasters, family dissensions, personal failures.

Martin Roy's address was a squat, ugly stucco rooming house that had once had a paint job, but not in my lifetime. The entrance was a warped screen door, through which I could barely see a short, dim hallway with cracked brown walls and dark doorways. I rattled the edge of the door with my knuckles.

A man materialized from the darkness of a doorway in back and lumbered toward me through the gloom of the hall. A tall, bulky man with long arms and shoulders that stretched under his sports shirt like basketballs. He got closer and I made out dirty white hair and an old, seamed, long-jawed face. A plug of chewing tobacco made a knot in his right cheek. Past plugs had left stains on his lips and the gray stubble over his chin.

He halted and squinted at me through the rusty, soot-blackened screen. "Yeah?"

"Martin Roy in?"

"Who?" His pale eyes watched me stonily. He didn't dislike me. He didn't know me.

"Martin Roy," I repeated.

He studied me some more before answering: "Ain't here. Ain't been here ten-eleven months."

"Where'd he go?"

The shoulders moved in a slow shrug. "How would I know? He just moved out."

I made myself patient. He was the kind who liked to take simple questions and study them for hidden content. "Are you the super here?" I asked him.

He even had to think about that before deciding the answer wouldn't hurt him. "Uh-huh. That's me."

I got a five-dollar bill out, wrapped it around my thumb, and told him, "I'd like to get in touch with Martin Roy. Wherever he is."

His eyes dropped to my interesting thumb, jumped back to my face. "Why?"

They don't believe in reporters in neighborhoods like that. They know that man-hunters come in only three varieties, all three of which it is better to have nothing to do with. Cops mean trouble, hoods smell of death, and private detectives are from collection agencies after long-unpaid bills.

I tried a stab in the dark. "I want some pictures from him." It wasn't anything I couldn't slip out of if it didn't mean anything to the super.

It meant something to him. "He still takin' pictures? Always locked up in the bathroom when somebody needed to use it, developing those films of his. I yelled at him about it, but he said it was the only place he could use as a darkroom. When he stained the sink and tub with those chemicals of his, I told him to get out. Never did pay his rent on time, anyway."

I scratched the five-dollar bill across the screen between us. "Where's he live now?"

"I wouldn't know." He eyed the bill scratching at the screen. "How much is that?"

"Five."

"Make it more and maybe I'll ask around after my nap, see if anybody knows where Roy moved after I kicked him out."

"It's worth twenty dollars to me, to get in touch with him."

The super pulled the screen door open. "Okay. I'll see what I can do for you." He held out a calloused palm.

"After I get in touch with Martin Roy." I put the five back in my pocket, got out my business card, and dropped it in his waiting hand. "Call me if you locate him."

He took a long time to read the few words and phone number on the card. "Private dick. So that's what you are."

"That's right. I want Roy to take some photos to help in a divorce case."

"So you say. Could be something else. You could be lookin' to make trouble for him, some way."

"If I am, would you care?"

He thought about that. "No. Guess not. But how do I know you'll pay up, after I go to all the trouble of askin' around?"

"I have to go on working in this town. I'd run out of co-operation if word got around I didn't pay what I owed for information."

He thought some more. "Yeah . . . that's so. Well, like I said, I'll ask around."

I had to leave it that way. Going into a bar at the end of the block, I found a phone booth in back and checked through the phone book. There was no listing for Martin Roy. On the off chance, I looked for Carol Branco. Nothing for her, either. I made calls—to a photo supply store, to a number of photographers I knew, and to three divorce lawyers who often used staged photographs as proof of infidelity. Nobody knew of a photographer named Martin Roy. All I got were promises to spread the word around that I was looking for him.

Putting the problem of Martin Roy aside for the moment, I called my office answering service. There was a message for me, from Mason in New York:

"The Jaguar with the license you gave me belongs to Dixie Snow, a stripper who works New York in the summers and Miami in the winters. She's working now at a club called The Golden Goddess, on Miami Beach. Kovac owes me thirty bucks. You only owe me twenty. An even fifty altogether. Fair enough?"

The Golden Goddess was in the bottom wedge of Miami Beach, between Collins and Ocean Drive. The owner, Marie Murphy, was an old poker-session friend of mine. I'd called, and she'd told me Dixie Snow was at the club with her, training a new girl. It was three in the afternoon when I got there.

The neon sign outside was in the shape of a nude woman with her arms outstretched in welcome. By night it glowed yellow, acquiring some life. By day it was just so much neon tubing. Inside the entrance was a statue covered with shiny gilt, a plaster copy of the Venus of Milo. The front room was empty except for Moe the bartender and a lone male customer hunched dejectedly over a tall Bloody Mary. The door to the club's main room was closed. It didn't open until eight at night, an hour before the first show.

Moe looked at the bandage on my forehead. "Hi, Tony. Business a little rough these days?"

The lone customer turned his head to look at me, and I saw why he was dejected. He had an angry first-day sunburn that would keep him inside the next few days and make his nights a torment.

"Rough enough," I told Moe. "Murph in back?"

"Yeah. Go on through. She's expecting you."

The main room was large and circular, crowded to the limit with clusters of chairs around postage-stamp tables. It was dim inside, the only lights that were on being at the far end, on either side of the tiny stage. At one side a piano player was fingering something from Debussy. Marie Murphy sat cross-legged on one of the tables near him, watching the two girls on the stage.

One wore an extremely tight black leotard that displayed her voluptuous body with a nerve-knotting impact that sheer nakedness couldn't have achieved. She was tall, with long black hair and her face was masked by dark sunglasses. She was instructing the other girl, a medium-sized redhead in a modest skirt and blouse, who was moving around a clear-plastic bathtub in time to the music while she unbuttoned her blouse. Her movements were unpracticed and self-conscious. She looked like a pretty college freshman, not the sort of girl who'd take off her blouse in public. Which was what gave some excitement to her amateurish performance, and was probably the reason they were taking the trouble with her.

I announced my presence by rapping lightly on a table top. Marie Murphy turned her head, saw me and waved a hand. She said something to the girl in the black leotard, who said something to the other girl. The redhead nodded and went on with what she was doing. She'd dropped her blouse and was unzipping her skirt. It fell, and she leaned over in a chaste white slip to test the imaginary water in the tub with a finger. The water was supposed to be too hot. She jerked it back and sucked at it with pursed lips, her big, innocent eyes gazing blindly at where the audience would be. She resumed her prowl around the tub, trying hard to match her movements to the piano music. The girl in the black leotard left the stage and came across the room toward me.

She came into the gloomy part of the room, her hips bumping against chairs and tables on the way. She had the hips to bump them with.

"Damn!" she whispered as she reached me. "It's so dark back here." She rubbed the sore places with her hands.

"Wouldn't be so dark if you took off the sunglasses."

"Couldn't see at all without them," she explained. "They're prescription lenses . . . Murph says you're a friend of hers and you wanted to see me about something."

"That's right. Mind taking off the glasses a minute?"

"What for?"

"I want to see what you look like."

She took off the sunglasses and peered at me nearsightedly. She had the sort of pushed-in pekinese face Brigit Bardot made popular. Not at all like the blonde in the silver-framed portrait in Mrs. Branco's house.

"Okay?" she asked.

"Fine. You are Dixie Snow?"

"That's me." She put the dark glasses back on. "You looking to hire me for a stag party or something?"

"Do you own a red Jaguar with New York license plates?"

The question alarmed her. "Why? Something happen to it? If they've gone and wrecked it I'll . . ."

"Who're they?"

"The ones Murph loaned it to. She said some friends of hers needed my Jag for a month, paid me enough to make it worth my while. But if it's been in a smash-up . . ."

"It hasn't. I'm just trying to find out who's using it these days."

"Oh." Dixie calmed down. "You scared me for a minute."

"Who're these friends of Murph's?"

"Search me. Whyn't you ask her?"

"Do you know a Carol Branco?"

"Uh-uh."

"How about Martin Roy?"

"Doesn't ring a bell. They the ones using my Jag?"

"Maybe. Will you tell Murph I'd like some words with her?"

"Sure." Dixie Snow raised a hand in farewell. "See you around, maybe?" She maneuvered her way back toward the stage, her shapely, black-sheathed buttocks clenching and unclenching with an effect that she knew all about.

The redhead on the stage was down to white bra and panties. She had a nice, healthy figure. I watched her test the imaginary water again and find it to her liking. She straightened, facing out from the stage, and took off her bra. Her hands went to the back of her head in a pretense of tucking her hair up, making the firm globes of her breasts sway.

Marie Murphy came up beside me and asked, "Think she'll do?"

"She's pretty enough. Her first time?"

"Uh-huh. You never know with that type until there's an audience. Some of the innocent-looking ones clutch the boys by the throat, others leave 'em cold. Worst trouble with this one is, she doesn't know how to wiggle her rear. Look."

I looked toward the stage again. The redhead had her back to us and was stepping out of her panties. It was a fine, trim back, properly rounded and dimpled in the right places. She climbed into the tub, pretended to wash herself. Her figure was visible in profile through the clear plastic of the tub.

"See what I mean?" Murph said. "No wiggle. What's *your* problem?"

I returned my attention to Marie Murphy. She was a big, solid woman in her mid forties. When she'd been younger and less solid, she had done quite well for herself as a stripper under the name of Dazzle Dare. Her face was still pretty, if a bit plump. Overeating had caught up with her in her early thirties, but by then she hadn't given a damn. Unlike most, she'd saved the money she'd made in her slimmer days.

"It's that red Jaguar you borrowed from Dixie Snow," I told her. "Who has it?"

Murph backed off and rested her ample rear on the edge of a table. "Trouble?"

"For somebody. Who're these friends you gave the car to?"

"No friends of mine," she said bitterly. "They're the protection guys."

I waited. She studied me worriedly. Finally she said, "You're a friend and all, but I don't know what's going on. For all I know, if it gets around I told you, I could maybe get a face full of acid."

"It won't get around."

She worried some more before giving in. "Okay, Tony, but you remember. Anything happens to me, it'll be your fault."

"Murph, when'd you ever hear I was a blabbermouth?"

"That's true enough; you ain't. . . . So all right. So these two hoods walked in here one day and asked for a car. The red Jag was out front. They gave me four-hundred bucks to borrow it from Dixie for a month. I gave her the dough, she gave me the keys to the Jag, and they went off with it. That was over three weeks ago. Ain't seen them or the Jag since.''

"Why'd they want it?''

"They didn't say. And I didn't ask. With guys like them, that's the only safe way to be. I don't know what's going on. I don't want to know. Not from you, either.''

"What're their names?''

"They didn't mention names. And like I said, I've never seen them since.''

"You gave them what they wanted. Did they make threats?''

Murph gave a low, harsh laugh. "Not them. They didn't have to. They're that kind. The kind that comes in and tells you politely what to do. And you fall all over yourself in your rush to do it. So they'll stay polite. I've met enough of their kind in my time to spot 'em a block away. The sort that'd kill you as easy as swatting a fly. After they left I had myself two double bourbons. And you know, Tony, I ain't much of a drinker.''

"What'd they look like?''

"One was taller than you, bigger in the shoulders. I'd give odds he could take you, barehanded. Handsome devil. Something wrong with his leg. He limped a little.''

"Blond?''

"Yeah. . . . The other guy's smaller. About my height, and skinny, but even scarier than the big one. Nothing out of the ordinary about him, except his way of looking at you. And that soft voice.''

"What's his coloring?''

She thought back. "Average. Brown eyes and dark brown hair.''

So it was the same two that had smashed Lou Kovac. I mentioned the names Carol Branco and Martin Roy. They didn't mean anything to her. She was relieved when I took my departure.

At the door I looked back. The redhead was climbing out of the tub, her back to the audience. Dixie Snow tossed her a towel. The redhead pretended to be drying herself.

Murph was right. No wiggle.

Chapter 13

I CALLED THE STATE POLICE HEADQUARTERS OUTSIDE COF-fin City, said who I was and asked for Lieutenant Waine. He came on with news for me.

"It was Hurley's killing that woke you up last night, all right. Medical examiner pins his time of death to a twenty-minute period around two a.m. Also, we took a .32 slug out of his heart, and Hurley's .32 hasn't been found."

"Seymour Peck has a .32," I told him. "So does Serena Ferguson."

"I'm way ahead of you. Ballistics already checked their .32s. Neither one fired the slug we took out of Gil Hurley. You have a special reason for thinking it was one of them that did it?"

"No. It was just a thought. I don't expect it to be that easy."

"It never is," Waine said. "I got another piece of news for you. There's been a confession."

I frowned suspiciously at the phone. "To Hurley's murder?"

"Uh-huh. Surprising, isn't it?"

"Who confessed?"

"An old alcoholic beach bum named Joe White. Says he was wandering along the beach last night and came across Gil Hurley at the Coffin estate boat dock. He asked Hurley for dough to buy liquor, and Hurley got insulting and struck him. They wrestled. Hurley pulled his gun, but in the tussle got shot himself with it. Joe White tossed the gun in the ocean, he doesn't remember where. He says he didn't mean to kill Hurley, it was an accident.''

"Is Hollis Cobb the one who dug up this beach bum and got the confession out of him?" I asked dryly.

"You catch on fast."

"You believe this confession?"

"Nope. Neither do you, I take it."

"Neat trick to fool the voters," I said. "Cobb knew how bad it looked for him, his rival for Police Chief getting murdered just before election time. So he finds himself a patsy, fast. The voters are pacified because they've been handed a confessed murderer who doesn't have anything to do with the Tallant crowd. And Cobb improves his reputation as an efficient, quick-acting cop. After he's elected, the beach bum can go back on his confession, say he was muddled in the head when he made it. Reasonable enough for an old alcoholic.''

"Sure. With a retracted confession, and no evidence that he killed Hurley, the bum walks out scot free."

"At least that's what Cobb probably promised him," I said. "Along with plenty of future drinking money. What does this do to your end of the investigation?"

"Keeps us from pressing it inside Coffin City pretty effectively," Waine told me glumly. "We'll continue to do what we can outside town limits, of course."

"Has Willa Hurley pulled herself together enough to talk to?"

"Yeah. She doesn't believe the confession either. She's convinced her husband was killed by someone working for Tallant. And she's more determined than ever to smash Tallant. The *Clarion* is putting out a special edition tomorrow, with her financing. Serena Ferguson's going to fill it with the story of Hurley's murder, an announcement that Seymour

Peck is the reform group's new candidate for Police Chief, and a strong hint that the beach bum's confession is a phony."

"Any luck so far with Carol Branco?"

"No. She still hasn't showed up at her motel, and we haven't located her or her red Jaguar anywhere else."

"You'll keep looking?"

"Naturally. What'll you be doing?"

"Same as you," I told him. "Looking for Carol Branco."

I hung up and studied the phone for a time, thinking about what was happening in Coffin City. I decided to stir the pot a little more. My best chance of playing my hand to a win lay in disturbing whoever had the answers enough so they'd come after me. I put through a call to Serena at the *Clarion*.

She came on the phone full of excited energy. "Tony! Where'd you disappear to? I could have used your advice. I'm putting out a special issue of the *Clarion* tomorrow. All about what's happened."

"So I hear. Is there still time to get something new into it?"

"I guess so. What is it?"

"Do a story about the fact that Lou Kovac was investigating Tallant and Cobb and their group for the reform party. And what happened to him. Say I've taken over his investigation. Quote me as saying I'm certain the murder confession Cobb got out of that beach bum is a fake and a cover-up— and that I expect to be able to prove it soon."

"We can use that," Serena told me eagerly. "Front page. But isn't it likely to make trouble for you?"

"I live on trouble."

She laughed. "That's obvious. It's the one thing I sensed in you from the start. I suppose that's what makes you exciting." She stopped, then said in a softer voice, "That sounds very forward of me, doesn't it."

"Just sounds like you're all hopped up. Who do you think really killed Hurley?"

"Well, it certainly seems likely it was one of Hugh Tallant's men. Wouldn't you say so?"

"And if it wasn't—who then?"

"I . . . don't know."

"Are you sure?"

"You sound as though you don't believe me."

"You lied to me before," I said. "About you and Hurley."

There was a pause at the other end. "You saw Gil kiss me, that day you first came to the house."

"Uh-huh."

"It didn't mean what you think, Tony. There's been nothing between Gil and myself since he married Willa. I told you the truth about that. I admit I was disappointed when Gil dropped me to marry her. But I got over it. I certainly haven't been carrying any torch for him all this time. Gil just dropped by that day to thank me for my editorial. And . . . in the process he kissed me. So what?"

"Pretty ardent kiss, for just a thank-you."

"It didn't mean anything," Serena insisted. "It . . . Gil was like that. Exuberant." She shifted the subject: "Where are you calling from?"

"Miami."

"Oh. . . . But you'll be back?"

"Probably."

"I'd like to see you again," she said, hesitantly.

"Most likely you will, sooner or later."

I placed the phone back in its cradle, went out, and started hunting.

It was in one of the swankier Miami Beach hotels. The bronze plate on the blond door read: *Hanson Cordel—Public Relations*. The reception room inside was gleaming modern with sky-blue drapes and rug. I told the receptionist I'd phoned Hanson Cordel fifteen minutes earlier and that I had an appointment with him. She checked by phone and told me to go in.

Hanson Cordel's office was furnished like the reception room, with an entire wall of windows overlooking beach and ocean. The man who stood up behind the long pine desk was small and chesty, wearing a neat gray suit and a deep coat of Florida tan. He radiated vigor and sunshine.

"You're lucky to find me in," he told me cordially as he shook my hand. "I'm going to be late for a cocktail party. Business. But you said over the phone that it was urgent, so . . ."

He looked me over with a smile, trying to estimate if I was rich enough for my problems to be urgent for him, too. I showed him my credentials. He stopped smiling.

"Private detective? Is one of my clients in trouble?"

"I understand you conduct the Orange Growers' annual beauty contest for them."

"I *originated* the Miss Orange Juice contest."

"Remember Carol Branco?"

Cordel's manner became a bit cautious. "Yes, I do."

"I'm trying to locate her. Can you help?"

He leaned back in his chair, looking at me thoughtfully. "That's an odd thing," he said. "The contest Carol won was all of nine years ago. I haven't seen or heard of her since then. And now, within the space of weeks, there are two inquiries about her. Yours—and another man's."

"I'm trying to find her for her mother," I said. "What was this other man's reason?"

"He . . . said he was her brother. Also trying to find her."

"Carol Branco doesn't have a brother."

Cordel looked uncomfortable. "To tell you the truth, I didn't think so at the time. But I preferred to take his word for it. He wasn't the sort of man I'd care to have a violent argument with. And that's what any argument with him would have become, from the looks of him."

"What'd he look like?"

"A tall, blond man. Rather handsome and very strongly built. Like a weight-lifter or a pro fullback. But it was his manner that . . ."

"Did he have a limp?" I asked quietly.

"Yes—a slight limp."

"When was this?"

"A little more than a month ago."

I drew slow figure eights on his desk top with my finger. "What did you tell him?"

Cordel considered me for a moment. Then he told me, either because I looked honest, or because I looked like another one who might turn violent: "I said I lost touch with Carol Branco almost nine years ago, shortly after the contest. Which is the truth. We're not like the Miss America or Miss Universe contests, you know. We don't have last year's winner crown next year's, or anything of that sort. We just milk the contest for all it's worth for a week. Get stories and pictures of the girls sent out to papers all over the country, sometimes hit one of the national magazines. But after about a week it's done with. The winner takes her prizes and goes. I seldom have contact with them again."

"What's the last you know of Carol Branco?"

"The prizes that year were a thousand dollars cash, an all-paid round trip to Havana for two weeks, and a screen test with a Miami movie outfit that does advertising films. She had her vacation in Havana, and when she came back she got her screen test. I understood from Sol Fuller, who runs the movie company, that the test was bad. She proved to be no actress. He couldn't use her in any of his company's work. And that's the last I heard of her."

"That all you told this other man who asked after her."

Cordel nodded. "That and the address at which she was living when she entered the contest."

"I'd like that, too."

He called his secretary on the phone, and she brought in a file card. I copied Carol Branco's nine-year-old address off it, and also wrote down the address of Fuller's Feature Films, the place where she'd flunked her screen test. Hanson Cordel did not seem sorry to see me leave.

There were a number of people in the hotel lobby. As a matter of habit, and because circumstances warranted it, I looked at all of them in the process of going out.

One of them was a slim, medium-sized man in a plain blue summer suit and a straw hat, sitting in one of the chairs reading a copy of *Look Magazine*. There was nothing unusual about him. He was as inconspicuous as a shadow on a cloudy day at high noon. I didn't pay any special attention to him. Not the first time I saw him.

The sign over the door had three big letters: FFF. And under them in smaller print: *Fuller's Feature Films*. It was a big, whitewashed cement-block building that had been converted from a truck garage into a studio. I pressed the bell. It was after five now, and all the employees had gone home. But my phone call had caught Sol Fuller in the process of closing up shop, and he'd agreed to wait for me.

The man who opened the door wore a short, graying Vandyke beard that made his narrow, high-strung face seem longer than it actually was. He was tall and thin, with narrow shoulders that drooped wearily inside his loud sports shirt. He said, "Rome?" and I nodded, and he said, "I'm Fuller," and shook my hand. His grip hinted at more strength than his frame showed you. "Come on in."

He led me through a wide corridor walled with plasterboard, past a shooting studio that took up most of the building, into a small screening room with a projection booth at one end, a wall screen at the other, and about ten folding chairs in between. We sat in two of the chairs and he smiled at me nervously.

"How's Cordel?"

"Looked all right when I left him," I said.

His smile became more ingratiating and anxious. "How

come I never get any business from him anymore? He still sore at me?''

"I wouldn't know. I've only met him once. Today.''

"You gave me the impression you worked for him,'' he said accusingly.

"Sorry. I wanted to be sure you'd stick till I got here.''

"Hell . . . I was hoping . . . Cordel's never forgiven me for botching that job for him.''

"When was that?''

"Couple years ago. Underwater sequence, for a resort client of his, in the Keys. I told him I could handle it. Never did an underwater sequence before, but I thought I could. Worst film I ever shot. A lemon, I admit it. Oh, well . . . what'd you want?''

"Know a photographer named Martin Roy?''

"No. What's he to do with me?''

"It was just a possibility. Both of you being in allied fields.''

"That what you wanted to talk to me about?''

"No. It's about Carol Branco.''

I guessed what was coming next. I wasn't wrong.

"Carol Branco,'' Fuller said. "That's funny.''

I didn't think so.

"There was another man around asking about her—oh, about a month ago.''

"Tall, powerfully built and blond?''

"Uh-huh. He walked with a limp. You know him?''

"I'm going to, sooner or later.''

"I wouldn't advise it,'' Fuller said. "He wasn't exactly a friendly type.''

"I'm a private detective, working at the moment for Carol Branco's mother. She wants to find her. Can you help?''

Fuller shrugged with his shoulders, arms, hands and eyebrows. "I don't know where she is now, if that's what you want.''

"Tell me whatever you do know about her. Anything might help."

"I don't know what to tell you." He paused and thought about it. "Carol was a real juicy girl. Good-looking as they come. But she couldn't act worth a nickle, and she didn't photograph right. I mean, she still looked pretty on film, but that hot sexy quality that was what made her different from a thousand other pretty girls didn't come across on the screen. The test was a bust. I had to tell her. She took it hard. Seems she'd always figured she had what it took to be a movie star. I hated to disillusion her. I even went out with her a few times—because I felt sorry for her, wanted to cheer her up."

"Sure. That hot sexy quality you mentioned didn't have anything to do with it."

Fuller sighed and fashioned a half-hearted grin. "You're right, of course. I'm a hypocrite. And me a married man with two teen-age kids. Do I sound ashamed?"

"No."

He leaned forward, resting his forearms on his knees and staring at the floor. "I'm not. I had it for her bad. Couldn't think of anything else when I was with her, and that was more than a few times."

"Where was she living at the time?"

He told me the name of one of the best older Miami Beach hotels. "She moved in after she came back from Havana. But the thousand bucks she won didn't last long there, and she began to get desperate when it was gone. I helped her out a little. I even thought about getting a divorce to marry her. But . . . well, it wouldn't have worked."

"What happened?"

"I never had the kind of dough for what Carol came to want. She had her first taste of high living—in Havana and at the Beach hotel. She was determined to go on living like that. The best of everything. Since she didn't have what it took to make it in movies, she said she'd make it some other way. Any way she could. Then this guy showed up. A big-time gambler she'd met in Havana. In the chips. Carol went off to live with him in Las Vegas."

"This gambler have a name?"

"Charles Gonzales."

I thought back. My forefinger traced a small X on my knee. I thought some more, and drew a tight circle around the X. "There was a gambler named Charlie Gonzales that got fished out of the Miami River some years back. Shot-gunned through the chest. The word around was that he'd hit a run of bad luck and had to borrow from an underworld loan shark. Then he had more bad luck and couldn't pay off."

Fuller nodded. "I heard about it. That was a year after Carol went off with him that he was found in the river. So I knew they must have come back here from Vegas."

"Did you look her up?"

"No. I'd had a year to get over her. I knew all seeing her again could do for me was mess up my life."

"You never saw her again?"

"Once I did. About two years ago. Not to speak to. I was just walking down Collins and spotted her riding past in an open convertible. She didn't see me. She was with another girl I knew. Marilu Vidrine. A call girl. I knew that because I'd used her once. For an advertising account executive from New York who was down here and threw some business my way. He wanted to buy a girl for the night. I asked around and got this Marilu Vidrine. Luscious—but she didn't have what Carol did. That smoldering volcano quality."

"Where do I find her?"

Fuller shrugged. "She was living at the Salem Arms, over in Bal Harbour, that time I got in touch with her for the account executive. But that was three years ago. Now, I don't know."

"Who put you in touch with her?"

"A camera man that worked for me at the time. Mike Rowe. But that won't help you. He went off to Europe more than a year ago, to see if he could break into directing feature films there. I haven't heard from him since, don't have the faintest idea where he is now.''

I leaned back in my chair, digesting the background he'd given me on Carol Branco. It wasn't what she'd been looking for when she left Coffin City, or what she said she'd found when she came back ten years later. What was emerging was a picture of a girl who'd gone the route of a lot of other no-talent girls who came to the big city with over-inflated opinions of the marketable value of their youth and good looks.

"Did you tell all this to the big blond with the limp?" I asked Fuller.

"Yeah. Maybe I shouldn't have. But he's not a man I'd care to say no to."

I talked with Fuller a while longer, without finding out anything else of interest. When I left his place it was still daylight, but the sun was low and losing its heat.

I was driving away from Fuller's studio when I saw the man again.

The one who'd been in the lobby of the hotel where Hanson Cordel had his offices. The slim, medium-sized man in the blue suit and straw hat.

He was standing in an alley entrance across the street from Fuller's studio, halfway down the block. He was still inconspicuous, but this was the second time I'd seen him and that was one time too many.

I'd already cruised past him before realizing I'd seen him before. Slowing the Olds, I pulled over to the curb at the end of the block. By the time I climbed out of the car, he had disappeared.

Undoing the button of my jacket for quick access to the Luger, I headed for the alley. He wasn't in it. I strode through to the other side of the block. He wasn't in sight there, either. All I saw was the back end of a car going around a corner and speeding away. A black Buick with a Virginia license plate.

I went back to my car and sat in it drumming my fingers on the steering wheel and thinking long thoughts about a pair of hoods. One of them easy to peg because he was big and blond and limped. The other not so easy, because he was average height and slim with brown hair that could hide under a straw hat, maybe. An ordinary-looking man—perhaps even inconspicuous. They'd used a black Buick when they'd had at Lou Kovac with baseball bats.

If I was right, he knew the route I'd be taking. His big partner had taken the same route a month earlier, tracking down Carol Branco.

I stuck to the route, cutting across the heart of Miami through heavy going-home traffic, heading for the Venetian Causeway, the nearest way across Biscayne Bay to Miami Beach. It turned out I wasn't wrong. Crossing Eighth Street, a black Buick with Virginia plates appeared a few cars behind me.

The surest bet was that he intended to tail me until I led him to some nice spot secluded enough for a killing. I decided to oblige him by cutting south toward some of the usually deserted back roads below Miami. Once there, I could let him catch up with me.

A few blocks farther, the heavy traffic abruptly canceled our plans. I'd just crossed an intersection when in-turning cars blocked off the street behind me. The inconspicuous man in the black Buick was caught in the jam.

Both sides of the narrow street were too parked-up for me to pull over and wait, even if I could have resisted the pressure of the traffic behind me. I did the only thing I could, circling two blocks and returning to the intersection. By the time I got there, the traffic jam had broken. The black Buick was gone.

I cruised around for ten minutes without spotting him. It didn't annoy me too much. I had a hunch he'd find me again, sooner or later.

As hunches go, it was a pretty good one.

Chapter 14

My visit to Bal Harbour was a bust. Marilu Vidrine had moved out of the Salem Arms a year before. Nobody in the plush apartment building could tell me where she'd gone, or knew enough about her to give me a lead on locating her now. Nor were they familiar with the name Carol Branco.

I looked through the lobby phone book. No Marilu Vidrine. There was a lot of loose change in my pocket. I used all of it on local calls. First I phoned various of my gambling contacts. They all knew about Charlie Gonzales. Some remembered a gorgeous blonde who'd been living with him after he returned broke from Las Vegas. No one knew what had happened to her after Gonzales went in the river. A man connected with the numbers racket in south Dade County gave me the address where Gonzales had been living at the time of his death.

My next series of calls went to bartenders, hotel bell captains and cab drivers—all of whom earned commission steering johns to call girls. None of them knew Carol Branco. A number knew of a call girl named Marilu Vidrine, but not what had become of her. A couple of them had heard she'd moved away to Tampa a year ago, and that she was now back and operating in Greater Miami. One of the bartenders I spoke to had heard something about a photographer named Marty Roy working for an organized blackmail-photo ring in Palm Beach some months back. But that was all he knew about it.

None of the people I called knew where I could find Carol Branco, Marilu Vidrine, or Martin Roy. They all promised to ask around for me. Before long I'd have half of Miami hunting for them. Eventually I was bound to hook one of the three.

The inconspicuous man wasn't in sight when I left the Salem Arms. No black Buick tailed me down though Miami Beach to the dazzling violet-and-white hotel into which Carol Branco had moved after winning the beauty contest.

It was another fruitless trip. Nobody in the hotel knew anything about Carol Branco. The hotel record showed that she had lived there for five weeks some nine years back. And that was all it showed.

I drove back across the bay and up to North Miami, where Charlie Gonzales had lived his last days. The escort I was expecting didn't materialize on the way. The address I'd gotten for Gonzales was a frame boarding house. The woman who owned it remembered the good-looking blonde who'd lived with the gambler as Mrs. Carol Gonzales. Whether they'd actually been married or not, she didn't know. The couple had had some kind of fight and Carol had moved out, about a week before Gonzales was shot-gunned.

The landlady didn't know where she'd gone or where she was now. After all, that had been eight years back. The cops had come around after Gonzales died, and she hadn't been able to tell them anything about Mrs. Gonzales either.

I gave her a quarter to let me use her phone, and called Art Santini. He checked on the Gonzales killing investigation and came back with the news that the men on the case had located Mrs. Carol Gonzales working as a B-girl in a joint in El Portal. She'd claimed to know nothing about the murder of Gonzales. Since there was nothing to indicate that she did, the cops had let her go. There was nothing further in the files concerning Carol Gonzales. The investigating detectives were certain that Gonzales was killed for welshing on a debt to a loan shark, but had never been able to tag anybody for the kill.

I drove to the joint in El Portal and found nothing but more frustration. The owner told me Carol Gonzales had quit after working in his place for over a year. He had no idea where she'd gone after quitting, nor with whom.

That left me with the address where she'd been living way back when she'd entered the beauty contest. It was getting to be dusk as I drove there, which made car-watching in my rear-view mirror more difficult. But I made quite certain I wasn't being tailed by a black Buick.

It was a ratty section of Miami next to the railroad freight yards. Where Carol Branco's old address should have been, there were two big warehouses. I got out of the Olds, searched around, and finally spotted it—a small cement-block tile-shingled rooming house down at the end of a long, narrow alley running between the two warehouses. I didn't like that alley. I went through its gloomy depths with a hand on my holstered Luger.

At the end of the alley was an open cement area where two ancient cars and a battered pickup truck were parked. I looked into each of them before going past them and ringing the doorbell. It was my day for frustration. The rooming house was under new management. The old management had gone back to Italy to live five years ago, and none of the present tenants had been there more than two years.

I was halfway back up the driveway alley when a black Buick with a Virginia license turned into its street entrance and came roaring at me head-on.

My legs froze as though my feet had sunk roots into the concrete under them. The front of the Buick hurtled toward me, filling the alley with only inches to spare. There was no escape on either side of me; just the sheer cement walls of the warehouses. There was no time to turn and run back out of the alley. The heavy onrushing car would smash into me and over me before I made it. If the car hadn't gone into low gear to turn into the alley, and if I hadn't already had my hand on the grip of the holstered Luger, there'd have been no time for anything.

I ripped the Luger up and fired. I didn't waste the precious split-second between life and death in aiming. I just pointed the gun and fired it, three times in rapid succession, as fast as I could squeeze the trigger.

The Luger did the rest, recoiling sharply into the heel of my palm each time it spat death, the three shots blending together loudly within the confines of the warehouse walls. Three small holes appeared in the Buick's windshield, about four inches apart, each hole sending out its own surrounding network of spiderweb cracks.

The Buick slewed sideways, the right fender crumpling against the cement wall. The whole right side scraped along the wall with a shrieking and tearing of metal and smashing of glass. It bucked to a halt with the front bumper touching my legs.

The slim, inconspicuous man hung forward in the front seat, his chest braced against the steering wheel and his chin resting on top of it. His straw hat had fallen off. There was a bullet hole just below the part in his dark brown hair. His eyes stared emptily at me through the ruined windshield.

Three hours later I was finishing a cup of black coffee in a diner half a block from the Dade County Courthouse when Art Santini trudged in and sat in the booth across from me.

"No luck," he said angrily. "None at all. No identification on him, nothing to check about him or his clothes. We've sent his prints to Washington. Maybe we'll find out who he is, at least."

"How about the Buick?"

"We checked the engine serial number. Turns out it was stolen in New Orleans six months ago. The license plates are phonies. Hand mades. We went through the car inch by inch.

Only old match covers, a pack of cigarettes. Didn't find anything to tie him to anybody or any place. We did find something, though—a couple baseball bats in the trunk.''

I put down my fork.

Santini nodded. ''Looks like you got one of the pair that beat up Kovac. That's something, anyway.''

''Not enough,'' I told him. ''That still leaves the other one. And the one who told them to do it.''

I drove down to Dinner Key and went aboard the *Straight Pass*. Tangerine was curled up asleep on the fishbox in the stern, which he wouldn't have been if there had been any strangers waiting for me inside my unlit cabin. That suited me just fine right then. I was in no mood for more. I required a night's rest. Without the prospect of unpleasant visitors dropping in unexpectedly while I was asleep.

That was one of the advantages of having a boat for a home: it was easy to insure uninterrupted privacy for any length of time. Tangerine woke and stretched himself as I started the engines. I detached the water, electric, and telephone lines, and tossed a chunk of bait fish onto the pier. The cat leaped out of the boat after it. I cast off from the pier and headed out across the dark swells of the moonlit sea.

For about an hour I cruised south along the coast, anchoring finally off a strip of mangrove jungle. I stripped and dived overboard for a long, relaxing swim. It drained much of the tension from me, but not all. I got a bottle of brandy from the galley and Conrad's *Mirror of the Sea* from the hanging bookshelf, and settled down on the bunk with them. I finished all of the book and half of the bottle before the gentle movement of the boat rocked me to sleep.

It was ten the next morning when I returned to Dinner Key. The first thing I did was call my answering service. There was a message for me to call one of the procurer-bartenders I'd talked to the day before.

My call got him out of bed.

"Jesus, man!" he moaned through the phone. "I figured you'd call back last night. This is a rotten time to wake up a guy that has to work all night. You could've waited . . ."

I cut him short: "Why'd you call?"

"Marilu Vidrine. I found out where she is for you. From Webber, my pusher. She uses him, too."

"She's an addict?"

"Oh, sure. Been hooked for years."

"Where do I find her?"

He told me.

Chapter 15

SHE LIVED IN A NEAT, NEW COTTAGE ON A QUIET, PLEASANT residential street in Coral Gables, not far from the University of Miami main campus. Before getting out of my car I reached under the dashboard and pulled loose the four-inch .22 automatic I kept taped there for emergency use. A little thing, but any one of the six shots in the self-ejecting clip could do effective damage at short range. I worked the top one into the fire chamber, stripped off the tape and thumbed off the safety. Slipping it out of sight inside the sleeve of my jacket, I made certain it was in tight enough not to fall out unless I wanted to shake it down into my hand. Just in case I was walking into something sticky.

I rang several times before the door was opened a few inches by a sleepy-eyed woman in men's striped pajamas. She was a tall, busty brunette in her thirties. Her ripe figure was on the verge of going sloppy, and her face was acquiring too much padding. She was still good-looking. Not as good-looking as she'd been a year before, perhaps; but better looking than she was going to be in another year. She had reached that time in her life when her way of life was abruptly taking its toll.

"For God's sake what d'you want?" she growled in a voice like sandpaper.

"Carol Branco," I told her.

Fear leaped into her eyes like flaming matches. Fear of

me. Her sleepiness vanished and she backed away a step.
"Oh . . . Well, come in but I can't tell you anything. . . . I
still haven't heard from her. . . . Honest!"

I stepped inside and shut the door. We were in a small,
expensively furnished living room. Marilu Vidrine backed
away some more, her legs shaky, her frightened eyes staying
on my face.

"I want Carol Branco," I told her menacingly, playing to
the unknown shape of her fear. "Don't make this hard on
yourself."

"I don't know where she is!" Marilu pleaded. "I *swear*
it. . . . Like I told your partner yesterday, I ain't seen Carol
in over three weeks, since she went away with him. And I
haven't heard from her. Not since yesterday, either. That's
the truth! I promised to tell if I found out where she is, but *I
haven't*. I can't tell you if I don't know, can I?"

"You claim you saw my partner yesterday?"

"Sure I did! The big blond guy."

"With a limp."

"Yeah. Him. Didn't he tell you?" She was looking puzzled. "He said he'd be back to see if I'd heard anything. Him
or a partner of his. . . ." Her voice slowed till it ran down.
I'd wakened her out of what was probably a doped sleep, and
she hadn't had time to do any thinking about it before. Now
she was beginning to. "You are his partner?"

"His partner's dead," I told her. "I killed him. I'm on the
other side of the fence—working against them."

The fear went out of her. Friendliness did not take its
place. She narrowed her eyes at me and hissed, "Who are
you? Cop?"

"Private detective." I got out my wallet and showed her
the photostat of my credentials. She hardly glanced at it,
being too busy trying to re-sort things in her mind.

"I don't get it . . ." she muttered. "You come here
and . . . What d'you want with Carol?"

"I have some questions that she has the answers to. If I

find her first, I can protect her from that blond friend of your with the limp. I'd lay three to one that if he finds her first, nobody'll ever see her again."

Marilu sat down on the edge of a sofa and made fists on her pajama-clad knees and stared down at them. "Yeah," she whispered, half to herself. "I think you're right. He didn't say so . . . but I got that feeling . . ."

"Where is she?"

She didn't say anything for some time. When she looked up at me her face was wooden, uncommunicative. "I don't know," she said flatly.

"Who's the blond guy with the limp?"

"I don't know."

"Tell me about that time three weeks ago—when Carol Branco went away somewhere with him."

She looked at me hard eyed. And said nothing.

"You'll have to tell me what you know," I said.

"And get myself killed?" She shook her head heavily. "You can't make me say anything. I don't know anything to tell you."

"You can tell me about Carol Branco. And why she went away."

"Carol who?" Marilu drawled, her decision firming. "I don't know anybody named Carol."

I let my breath out slow. "If it has to be this way," I said softly, "then it has to." I took hold of her left hand and raised it off her knee. She didn't understand at first. But when I pushed her sleeve up over her elbow she did. There were needle marks up and down the inside of her arm. New ones, recent ones, the scars of old ones.

I dropped her arm and told her gently, "I'll throw you to the narcotics squad if I have to."

Fear leaped into her eyes again. "W-what?"

"You ought to go someplace where they can help you kick the habit, anyway. But the way the cops do it isn't the easiest way. For a while there, you'd rather be dead. Maybe you've heard about it.''

I saw she had, and pressed the point. ''That's what you'll go through if I call the narcotics boys and turn you in as an addict. They'd like the idea of putting a call girl out of business at the same time. And they'd take you off the heroin completely the minute they got their hands on you. None of the business of weaning you off it gradually. Don't force me to do that to you, Marilu.''

She stared at the floor, chewing on her knuckles and saying nothing. I reached for the phone on the table next to her sofa. She grabbed my wrist with both hands.

''Please!'' she whispered despairingly. ''Don't . . . I couldn't stand it. Not that way. Not cold turkey . . . with nothing to take the edge off. . . . I'd go crazy. I know I would. I've tried to kick the habit by myself that way. Even drinking whisky till it came out of my ears I couldn't do it. I just got sick . . . awful sick . . .''

''Where's Carol Branco?''

She let go of my wrist and leaned her forearms on her knees, her body drooping. ''I don't know,'' she whispered wearily. ''Honestly I don't.''

''Who's the blond man with the limp that she went away with?''

''I don't know his name or anything about him. That's the truth . . . Carol didn't say anything about him.''

''What do you know?''

Her nervous fingers plucked and twisted at the striped material of her pajama pants. Her strained eyes came up to mine, pleading. ''You'll get me killed, mister. They'll kill me for this—I know they will.''

''They?''

''The blond guy, and his partner.''

''He doesn't have a partner any more,'' I said. ''I told you what happened to him.''

''Sure. You told me. How do I know it's true?''

"It was in the early editions of the morning papers."

Marilu looked toward her television set. There was a folded newspaper on it. "I picked one up around three this morning. On my way home. Haven't read it yet."

I got the paper and opened it to the item about the attempt of an unknown man to kill me with a stolen Buick. I dropped it in her lap, pointing to the story. "Read all of it." The final paragraph of the news story said that the police believed the unknown man I'd killed was one of the two men who'd beaten up a private detective named Louis Kovac. It said the police were still hunting the other man, described as tall, blond, powerfully built, and walking with a slight limp.

Marilu read it, and dropped the paper to the floor at her feet. "That still leaves the blond guy. He's a torpedo—I know the type. A killer."

"He won't be able to do you any harm if I get him first. And Carol Branco can get me to him. Start talking."

The strain was getting to all of her now, making her tremble. "Wait a minute, will you?" She started to get up. "I have to go to the bathroom."

I pushed her back down, gently. "No. After we talk about Carol Branco."

"You don't understand . . ." Marilu blurted.

"I do, though. You want to shoot yourself full of heroin. It'll have to wait."

"But I need it! I got to have a fix first thing in the morning or my nerves go to pieces!"

"You'll have it soon enough," I told her. "As soon as you tell me all about Carol Branco."

She seized her face in her hands, her fingers digging into her eyes. I sat on the edge of a chair, positioning myself so I could watch her, the windows, the front door and the doorway to the rest of the cottage at the same time. I laced my fingers together between my knees, watching her and waiting. It wasn't pleasant; but it was the only way to get the truth out of her.

I got it—in bits and snatches, her voice going ragged and beginning to shake. She'd known Carol Branco for several years. They'd become friends through their both being call girls, and both having a heroin addiction.

"She told me once her real name was Branco," Marilu said. "But that's not the name she used. Called herself Carol Shelley. Just in case the cops ever picked her up and it got in the papers. She's got a mother still living. She didn't want her to hear about it."

"Did she ever mention Charlie Gonzales to you?"

"Sure. She lived with him for a year."

"Were they married?"

"No. . . . He took her to Vegas with him. They lived high, had a great time, she said. But then he went broke, That's how Carol got into the call-girl business. Gonzales shoved her into it, to make dough for him to gamble with. But he kept losing. They came back here to Miami, and it was more of the same. She got sore about peddling her body and having him take everything she made and lose it. So she walked out on him."

"She ever tell you who killed Gonzales?"

"She said she didn't know—and didn't care. Then a year later she met another guy she went for. A big bandleader. Went off on the circuit with him around the country. He's the one got her on H. He was a user, so he got her hooked to keep him company. They stuck together a real long time, but then he decided to take a cure, and made her take one, too. His took, hers didn't . . . and after that they couldn't make it together so they broke up. It was right after that I met her."

"Here in Miami?"

"Yeah . . ." Marilu stopped, fighting against the ravages of her dope-craving nervous system. Her hands wouldn't stay still, kept pulling at her knees and clawing her palms. I waited, and she finally went on in a jerky voice: "She had a big habit to feed, and once she was on her own again, there was only one way she could get up that much dough every

day. So she went back to being a call girl, and . . . that's
how we got to know each other. Got to be pretty good friends.
Then I went off to Tampa with a guy that got a thing for
me. . . . Big insurance salesman. . . . Put me up in a flossy
apartment there—till his wife found out about it. . . . He
didn't want a divorce, so he stopped paying my rent and I
came back here. . . . Ran into Carol again, and we decided
to save dough by living together. Moved in here."

"When was this?" I asked her.

"Six-seven months ago. Worked out pretty good—except
when she'd have one of those fits of depression. Then it was
awful. I couldn't stand being in the same house with her but
I'd be scared she'd cut her wrists or something if I left her
alone."

"What was she depressed about?"

"Everything, when she, was in one of the black moods
. . . being on dope, being a call girl, everything. Kept saying
how she could've married a nice guy, but she'd jilted him to
make the big time, and she'd never expected to end up like
this . . . crap like that . . ."

She suddenly lunged to her feet and started a wobbly run
out of the room. I shot off the chair, caught her arm and
dragged her to a halt. Marilu swung around toward me, her
face twitching uncontrollably. "I gotta have a fix!" she
screamed at me. "You don't know how it hurts!"

"Then stop stalling," I told her tightly. "You keep talking
about everything else except what I'm after. Tell me about
the blond hood with the limp. Then you can have your stuff."

She was breathing hard, struggling to hold on to the shreds
of control. In a minute I'd have to pull her down off the walls.

"All right, damn you!" she blurted. "He came around
here one day . . . almost a month ago . . . Talked to her in
private, where I couldn't hear . . ."

"Did she act like she knew him?"

"She didn't know him . . . not before he came here that
day. . . . But she went off somewhere with him. Came back

late that night . . . driving a red sports car and wearing a gorgeous mink. . . . She said the blond guy gave 'em to her . . . that she had to go off for a couple of weeks to do a job for him. . . . Wouldn't say who he was or where she was going or anything. . . .''

"Was she happy about what she was going to do for him?"

"Hell, no! She was in . . . one of those lousy black moods again . . . but scared of something, too. . . . Didn't stay long enough for me to find out anything . . . just came back for some of her clothes—and a fix. Took along the rest of her supply. . . . She didn't have much, but she said it was all right. Somebody was gonna keep her supplied with the junk for free while she was away. . . . She should've known better. You can never depend on anybody else when it comes to your supply. I told her that last night when . . .''

Marilu's voice dragged to a stop. She stared at me in shock, realizing what she'd let slip. It would never have happened if I'd allowed her to have her fix before she started talking.

"That's fine," I said thinly. "Now tell me the rest of it."

Marilu just went on staring at me, frozen.

I let go of her arm and picked up the phone and dialed headquarters. Holding the phone out to Marilu, I let her hear the desk sergeant who picked up the phone at the other end. Then I put it to my ear and told the sergeant to get me Bill Phillips in Narcotics.

Marilu slammed her hand down on the phone cradle, cutting the connection. She told me brokenly, "Carol's at a beach cabin I own north of Fort Lauderdale."

I lifted her hand off the cradle and put the phone down in its place. Marilu collapsed on the sofa and buried her face in her trembling hands. I stood over her and waited.

"It's a place a guy gave me as a present a few years back," Marilu said finally, her voice so low I could barely make out the words. "I keep some of my clothes there . . . go there sometimes when I'm in the mood and loaf around in the sun for a few days. . . . Took Carol with me sometimes. She

knows where I keep the spare key under the doorstep. . . .
She phoned me from there last night. . . . Said she was in
bad trouble. That she was sure somebody was after her and
they'd kill her if they found her—to shut her up.''

''Shut her up about what?''

''She didn't say. . . . She was talking real wild, scared
stiff. . . . Said she needed a fix bad, and she didn't have any
of her H with her. And she was afraid to go to her regular
pusher, because they'd know she needed the stuff and they
might be waiting there for her.''

''Who're *they*?''

''She didn't tell me that. . . . I told you, she was wild, not
making sense half of the time. . . . She wanted me to bring
her up some of my heroin caps. . . . I told her I couldn't. . . .
I was scared to. I told her about the big blond guy coming
around yesterday afternoon wanting to know where she
was. . . . He warned me not to help her. If I found out where
she was, I was supposed to wait and let him or his partner
know when they came back today. . . . I wouldn't've done
that. . . . But I didn't have the nerve to take any caps up
there to her. Suppose one of them was keeping an eye on me
and tailed me there? He'd kill me, too!''

''What else did Carol tell you?''

''Nothing. . . . Just that she didn't know what she was
gonna do now . . . where to go. . . . She needed a fix, and
she was scared they'd find her, and . . . well, then she started
crying and hung up.''

''Hear from her again?''

''No. I felt lousy about not helping her, but what could I
do? I want to go on living, too!''

I looked at the phone and scratched my jaw, and finally
decided calling Carol Branco wouldn't be the right way. Even
with Marilu doing the talking, it might start her running
again.

''Get your clothes on,'' I told Marilu. ''You're taking me
to that beach cabin.''

While she vanished into the bathroom, I went into the kitchen and boiled a pot of strong coffee, set out two cups. When Marilu came into the kitchen she was a different girl. The blouse and skirt she'd put on displayed her figure more flatteringly than the men's pajamas had. And the needle full of heroin she had pumped into her veins had firmed her face and given her a certain amount of temporary courage.

We finished off two cups of coffee apiece, black. Then we went out to my car and drove north. The tiny .22 automatic was still stuffed up the sleeve of my jacket. I left it where it was, just in case.

North of Fort Lauderdale we turned east to a colony of cinder-block cabins with red tile roofs, set apart along the edge of the sand. The cabin Marilu directed me to had a cluster of high, flowering bushes fanning out from its left wall. I drove down a narrow dirt path and around the bushes. There was a red Jaguar parked there, next to the cabin.

We got out of the Olds and Marilu led the way up onto the cabin's small porch. She knocked at the door and we waited. There was no response.

Marilu looked relieved. "She's not here."

"Her car is." I reached past her and tried the knob. It wasn't locked.

Elbowing Marilu aside, I opened my jacket and drew out the Luger. I pushed the door open, hard, taking two fast steps inside.

The interior of the cabin consisted of one big plainly furnished main room and a bathroom. The main room contained a small kitchenette. There was a studio couch against the right wall, and another against the left wall that had its spread off and was made up as a bed. Somebody had slept in it.

The only one in the room was a blonde girl in a cashmere sweater and plaid skirt, sprawled on her back in the middle of the plank floor, next to a pine chair.

Her arms were outflung, her slim hands slightly curled. One of her legs was twisted under the other. There was a dark bruise on one shin. Her feet were bare. Even in death there was no mistaking her face—the same face I'd seen in the silver frame in her mother's house. Carol Branco.

"Oh, God . . ." Marilu whispered behind me. "He found her—*here*. Now he'll figure I was holdin' out on him."

I went to one knee beside Carol Branco. By the feel of her, she'd been dead for hours. There was a dark bruise on her right cheek and smaller bruises on her throat. As though someone had hit her and tried to strangle her. But what she'd died of was a bullet through the brain.

Whoever had killed her had put the muzzle of a gun against her left temple as the trigger was squeezed. There were contact powder burns around the hole the slug had drilled into the side of her head. The bullet hole itself was small.

Small enough to have been made by a .32.

Chapter 16

THE NOON WIND WAS PICKING UP, CHURNING WHITECAPS over the surface of the ocean, driving long rollers onto the beach and kicking up sand. I sat on the porch steps and watched. It had gotten crowded inside Marilu's cabin—what with State and County cops and lab men, plus the County assistant D.A. I was finishing a Lucky when Lieutenant Waine came out and sat beside me, wiping a hand across his rugged face.

"I just phoned Carol Branco's mother," he said. "She's driving down."

"How'd she take it?"

"Like she didn't believe it. It's not gonna be fun, watching her find out it's true." Waine moved his big shoulders back and forth and gazed bleakly at the pounding surf. "Funny thing in there. This Marilu Vidrine says it's her clothes that Carol Branco's wearing."

I raised an eyebrow at him.

"Yeah. The cashmere sweater and the plaid skirt. Not the bra and panties under 'em."

"Any of Carol Branco's own clothes around?"

Waine nodded. "Slacks and sweater, hanging in the closet. Marilu identifies them as belonging to Carol Branco." He scratched the tip of his nose. "Well, maybe she just wanted a change. And the rest of her stuff is back in her motel in Coffin City. All she had with her was what she was wearing.

The slacks and sweater tally with what the clerk at her motel says she was wearing when she went out the other night."

"When you get the slug out of her," I told Waine, "check it against the one you took out of Gil Hurley."

He looked at me sharply. "You think they were killed by the same person?"

"Uh-huh."

"Keep talking."

I shook my head. "Don't know enough yet. First find out if I'm right." I dropped the stub of my cigarette in the sand, ground it under my heel and stood up. "If I'd gotten to Carol Branco while she was still alive, I'd have the answer. As it is, that leaves me the big blond with the limp, and Martin Roy. If I can find one of them."

"I put out an all-state check on Martin Roy," Waine told me. "All I've got back so far is a rumor he's been hanging around Palm Beach lately."

"Yeah, I heard the same rumor." I raised a hand in farewell. "I'll be calling you." I went to my car and drove to Palm Beach.

I spent the rest of the day prowling Palm Beach, getting nothing back for my time except that a man answering Roy's description had bought a lot of film for a Rolleiflex from one photo supply shop five weeks back. They didn't have an address for him.

· I treated myself to dinner at the best French restaurant in Palm beach, and sat a long time over my coffee and brandy putting things together. The trouble was, they fitted together several different ways. There was one large piece missing, in the center. Until I found it, I couldn't be sure.

Using the restaurant phone, I called Lieutenant Waine.

He came on with a question: "How'd you know?"

"The slugs match?"

"Sure do. Gil Hurley and Carol Branco were killed by the same .32. No doubt about it. Now tell me how you knew."

"I didn't. Just playing a hunch."

He chewed on that, not sure he believed me. Finally he growled, "Well—your hunches are a damn sight better'n mine. I figured whoever took Hurley's gun and shot him with it, would've gotten rid of it. Doesn't make sense, his carrying it around with him, taking a chance on getting caught with it."

I didn't say anything to that. Instead, I asked him, "When did Carol Branco die?"

"Medical examiner puts the time of her murder between midnight and one this morning. . . . By the way, I could've used your help later with that dame you turned up, Marilu Vidrine. She went all to pieces when Carol Branco's mother showed up and viewed the body. Not that I blame her. Mrs. Branco's one of the ones that doesn't cry, and you know how lousy that can be. She just stood there looking down at her daughter with a face like something out of a grave. I've seen 'em like that before, and it always gets me worse than when they break down. This Marilu was the one broke down. Acted like she was gonna go off her rocker."

I could guess why. Marilu had been overdue for her afternoon fix by then. "Where'd you take her?"

"Back to her house in Miami. I called Lieutenant Santini about it. He's got two men staked out around her place, in case that blond guy with the limp shows up. We still haven't had any luck finding him—or Martin Roy. How about you?"

"No luck at all."

I hung up and sat there moving a few of the pieces of my mental jigsaw puzzle around a little. The center piece was still missing. I thought I knew what the shape of it would be, but that wasn't knowing for certain.

I called my answering service to see if any of the inquiries I'd scattered around Miami the previous day had borne fruit. There was only a single message for me, from a man who hadn't left his name: "Be at your office at nine tonight. I'll call you."

There were still two hours to go till nine. But I couldn't think of anything constructive to do with them, so I drove back to Miami and went to my office building. Nobody was laying for me in the corridors. No guns fired at me from inside my office as I opened the door and snapped on the lights. I relocked the door, sat behind my desk and gazed at the wall. The wall remained a wall. Blank. No pictures flashed on it; no solutions materialized. I smoked and took the pieces of my puzzle apart and put them together again. They fitted the same way, with the hole in the middle. I looked through the windows at the night lights of Miami and listened to the night noises drifting up from the streets.

The phone on my desk rang at exactly nine o'clock. I picked it up and listened to somebody breathing at the other end.

After a while a man's jittery, high-pitched voice spoke in my ear: "Rome?"

"Uh-huh."

"This is Marty Roy," he said. "I get the word you been looking for me. What d'you want?"

"Information. Let's meet and talk."

"What about?"

"Carol Branco. And a tall blond man with a limp."

"Jerry?" he said, and then stopped himself. After a few seconds he said, "It'll cost you. How much is it worth to you?"

I ran a finger along the inner edge of my desk and gazed at the wall. "You name it."

There was more silence at the other end.

"Can you raise five hundred this time of night?" he asked.

"I can. Whether I give it to you depends on how much you can tell me."

"What I know's worth every cent of it." His case of jitters was getting worse. "How long'll it take you to raise the dough?"

"Less than an hour."

"Get it. I'll call you back at ten and tell you where to meet me. And no cops. You bring cops and I'll clam up. You won't get a word out of me."

"No cops," I promised.

He hung up. I put my phone down and lit a cigarette and waited. I'd lied about getting the money. His talk of needing it stacked up as so much bluff. About the cops I kept my word. I didn't call them. Wherever he was waiting for me, he probably wasn't waiting alone. But there was always the chance I was wrong. And if he was alone, I preferred to deal with him without interference. One way or another, I intended to get from him the identity of whoever was responsible for what had been done to Lou Kovac. It might not be a nice way.

I smoked two cigarettes. They tasted bitter. Or maybe it was me. I got up and paced. It didn't loosen any of the tight-wound tension squeezing me. I sat down and smoked some more. At ten the phone rang. It was Martin Roy again.

"You get the five hundred?"

"I have it," I told him.

"That's the ticket." His voice jumped with every syllable, as though someone were plucking his nerves. "There's an abandoned ship laid up in the river. An old coastal freighter. At the bottom of Don Street. Know the place?"

"I'll find it. Wouldn't it be simpler for you to come to my office?"

"You kidding? I'm taking a long chance as it is. I wouldn't do it even this way if I didn't need that dough to get away. I been holed up on that ship two days now, so I know it's safe. You meet me there or the deal's off."

"I'll be there."

"You can make it from your place in twenty minutes easy. Come any later and I won't be there." There was a click at the other end.

I put the phone down slowly, thinking about a river that drifted out of the Everglades to twist its way lazily through the heart of the city. It was a river with a lot of uses. There were plenty of rusting, rotting hulks abandoned in it; but there were also plenty of still-active vessels plying up and down it—by day. By day the river was a live, busy place, used by the industries, shipyards and boat docks crowding its banks. Not that the river was inactive by night. It was just quieter, and darker, and the activity was of a different nature. In the past five-year span, the Miami Harbor Patrol had found exactly twenty-eight bodies in its dark waters.

The foot of Don Street was on the south bank of the river. I drove toward the north bank. Whoever was on the abandoned ship would be watching Don Street, waiting for me to drive up there. I hoped.

I parked two blocks from the river and walked the rest of the way. The streets there were dark, lampless, the warehouses and factories around me shut for the night, their black looming walls cutting off the moonlight. I made my way toward a spot that was exactly across the river from the end of Don Street. The bank sloped down to the water between two closed buildings—an ice house and a wholesale seafood distributor. I stopped in their concealing shadows at the water's edge, looking across the river.

An ancient tramp freighter lay against the opposite bank, left there years ago to decay and eventually be broken up for cheap scrap metal. From the way it sat in the water, it was resting on the mud bottom. Which meant that it had been there long enough for its keel to rot open and let in the river. There were no lights on the ship. Its rusted hull and superstructure absorbed the moonlight, giving off no reflected glints. It looked like what it was: a dead ship.

I put my Luger in a plastic bag and wrapped it tight. Stripping to undershorts, I stuck the plastic-wrapped gun between my teeth and waded in. The turgid, muddy water was warmer than the night air. When I was neck-deep I shoved forward and began to swim, using a breast stroke to make no splash.

Keeping my legs below the surface, kicking carefully, I moved slowly and quietly across the dark river toward the other bank.

Halfway across, I stopped to tread water, studying the deck and superstructure of the dead ship to see if there was anybody on my side of it—the starboard side. Using my hands to keep the current from pulling me downstream, I stayed there till I had checked the vessel from bow to stern. There was no one in sight. As for someone being inside, observing my approach through a porthole—that much had to be left to luck, and wariness. The odds were with me that even if someone looked over the starboard rail, my head wouldn't be noticed moving in the waters below.

I swam nearer. The hull loomed large ahead of me, blocking my view of the south bank and its own superstructure above me. The abandoned hulk was heeled over slightly, resting its port side against the high bank. I reached the starboard side and swam silently along it to the anchor chain running down into the water from the bow.

When I grasped the chain with both hands, huge flakes of rust snapped off and dropped in the river. I hauled myself out of the water. More rust flakes fell, making splashes that tore at my nerves. I did a fast job of unwrapping the Luger and slipping my hand around its grip and my finger across its trigger, ready to fire. I looked up toward the bow deck and waited, my wet skin goose-pimpling in the cool air.

There was no sound aboard the ship. I told myself that the noises made by the falling rust flakes probably couldn't be heard from the height of the deck above. I told myself the ones waiting for me were most likely on the shore side of the ship, with the deckhouse between them and me to absorb any sounds I made. I told myself to stop shivering and start climbing. After a time I made myself do it.

Stuffing the plastic under the waistband of my shorts and putting the bare metal of the Luger between my teeth, I inched upward along the bulky links of the chain. Rust clung to my damp flesh and more of it dropped, but the splashes became faint as I got higher. I reached the top and went over flat, the length of my body pressing the rail. I dropped onto the forecastle deck, my bare feet making little sound on the rotting planks.

Crouching between the bulwark and cable winch, I took the Luger from my teeth and waited. My eyes, used to the darkness, could see into some of the shadows down the length of the deck. I studied each of them in turn. Most of all I listened. When I was ready, I moved across the forecastle and down to the forward well deck. My reception committee would logically be somewhere on the port side, amidship, looking down on the bank where Don Street ended. I kept to the starboard. Staying down close to the deck, I worked my way aft, following the concealing shadows of the two forward hatches and the cargo booms till I reached the midship deckhouse.

My safest course would be to get to a vantage point from which I could see all of the freighter's decks. Going up a ladder, I paused by the sagging lifeboat davits, then moved to an open door and peered into that level of the midship house. There was nothing inside but blackness. I couldn't even make out the passageways. Going up an iron stairway to the officers' quarters, I stopped again at a smashed porthole and listened for any sound inside. Hearing nothing, I went up the next ladder until I was up on the open flying bridge.

I crawled across it to the aft edge. For some minutes I studied the area between the house and the stern. When I was convinced no one was there, I moved to the port side of the bridge. From there I could look down on dark buildings cut through by the narrow band of Don Street reaching almost to the edge of the south bank. But my view of the decks directly below me was blocked by the port wing of the wheelhouse. I went back the way I'd come, silently. Climbing down to the starboard wing, I went through the dark wheelhouse and out onto the port wing. I went down to the next deck, held my breath, and leaned out cautiously over the rail.

Below me was the opening in the main deck rail where a gangway should have been. There was no gangway, but a Jacob's ladder hung over the side to the ground below. A man stood on the main deck at the top of the ladder.

He was a tall, lean man. Moonlight glinted off the glasses he wore. His attention was focused on the emptiness of Don Street. There was no one else in sight anywhere around him.

The possibility that he was actually alone didn't appeal to me as likely. I stayed where I was, waiting and listening, watching him watch the shore.

After a time, the man I was watching said, "Maybe he's not coming." His voice had a plaintive whine to it.

The voice that answered came from somewhere on the main deck directly below me. It was a low, heavy voice: "He'll come, Marty. Just stay where you are and wait."

Martin Roy turned around and said nervously, "Maybe he went to get some cops."

"He won't bring cops," the unseen man told him. "If he does, I just toss my gun into the river and then what can anybody prove? We're just two guys lookin' over an old wreck. Now shut your mouth and wait. He'll be showin' any minute."

"But he's late," Martin Roy pleaded. "Why would he be late if nothing's wrong?" He looked at his wrist. "Hell, I can't see the damn watch in this dark. But I know he's late." He looked up, toward the rising moon.

And saw me.

Chapter 17

I VAULTED OVER THE RAIL AND DROPPED FEET-FIRST, LAND-
ing on the deck beside Martin Roy as he yelled his warning.
I grabbed the front of his jacket in my left hand and twisted
around, getting the main deck rail against my back. The
other man was standing in an open doorway across the deck
from me. A giant of a man, with massive shoulders. I couldn't
see his gun in the shadows, but he had one. A heavy-caliber
one, from the roar that it made. He fired in the same instant
that I pulled Martin Roy's struggling form in front of me.

The slug smashed into Martin Roy's back and rammed
him forward against me. It must have killed him instantly.
His head flopped back as though his spine had been severed.
All of him became just so much dead weight hanging from
the jacket material bunched in my left fist.

The big man took two fast, long strides to his right, so he
could shoot at me without hitting the corpse I was holding.
He limped with each step. Moonlight glinted on his blond
hair.

I could have shot him then. But it was too shadowy for
anything except dead-center shooting, and I didn't want him
dead. Not yet. Not until he'd told me what I had to know. He
was the only one left now who could tell me.

So I didn't shoot. Instead, I threw Martin Roy's body at
him with all the strength I could muster. It rammed into him
and knocked him against the bulkhead. I sprang forward as

155

Roy's body spilled off him to the deck, and chopped my Luger viciously across his right wrist. He gasped, and his gun spun out of his sprung-open fingers and bounced away in the darkness somewhere.

I whipped the Luger up for a chop at his head. His left fist was faster. It exploded off my chest and hurled me backward. I caught my balance and jumped in the direction his gun had gone, expecting him to go after it. He didn't. Instead he leaped backward through the open doorway. I started after him. The heavy iron door clanged shut between us. There was the scraping noise of securing clips being turned inside, locking the door.

I ran to the nearest ladder, went up it to the next deck, and went inside. The passageway was pitch dark. I couldn't see an inch in front of my face. Putting my left hand against the cold metal wall, I felt my way forward till my fingers touched the rail of a ladder leading down. I waited there, listening for sounds below, clenching my teeth to still my breathing. Seconds dragged by, scraping my nerves raw.

There was the sound of shoe leather sliding across metal. But not below me. It came from somewhere above.

I moved quickly, following the handrail with my fingers till I felt another ladder leading up to the next deck. I went up the rungs swiftly and silently, still in total darkness, and came into the passageway there. Again I stopped and listened. There was no sound from him. But I sensed him there. Somewhere close to me. Either ahead or behind me. I waited a little longer, heard nothing. If he was there, he was waiting, too.

I chose the way ahead, moving one slow step at a time, holding the Luger waist high, ready to use it if I had to but hoping I could down him without killing. I reached the turning in the passage and felt my way warily around it. Every few steps I paused, straining my ears. My eyes were no good at all in that blackness.

After turning the next corner without running into him, I

began to get a prickling sensation at the back of my neck. I spun around, my finger stiffening across the trigger of the gun. He didn't jump me. If he was there, he was standing very still and not breathing, waiting for his chance.

Putting my back against the bulkhead, I moved sideways. That way I'd be ready for him, from whichever end of the passage he came at me. He didn't come at me. And I didn't bump into him. I turned another corner. Then another. That brought me back to where I'd started. He was no longer on that deck—unless he was stalking me. And he couldn't be, unless he could see in the dark.

Wherever he was, he eventually had to try getting off the dead freighter. I found the stairs and went down to the main deck. When I reached the bottom, I saw him.

His hulking figure was outlined hazily by the open doorway at the end of the passage. He was only a few feet in front of me, his back to me.

I brought the Luger up and said, "I've got a gun on you. Turn slowly." My voice sounded very loud in my own ears. It echoed through the empty ship.

He turned. I didn't see the fire ax in his hand till he swung it at me. By then it was too late to shoot him. I could have stood there and killed him on the spot and the swinging force of the ax would still have cut me in half. I sprang backward just in time. The slashing blade barely missed me. Its tip caught the barrel of the Luger and tore it out of my hand.

His laugh boomed in the confines of the passage as he came at me, swinging the ax again. I dodged sideways through a doorway and half fell, half ran down a flight of metal steps. I reached the bottom. His shoes clanked on the top steps above me. I started forward and blundered into a bulkhead, felt my way along it to another opening and went through it and down another flight of steps somewhere high inside the engine room. At the bottom of the steps my bare feet felt a level series of metal strips. It had to be a catwalk across the upper reaches of the engine room.

I followed it, feeling my way slowly and nervously with my bare feet. There were no handrails. That tramp had been built before safety precautions became law. One mis-step, and there'd be nothing but air under me until I hit the hard bottom far below.

It was darker there than it had been in the midships house. The darkness combined with the knowledge of huge emptiness below me to attack my sense of balance. Dizziness brought me to my senses. I went down on my hands and knees and crawled the rest of the way along the catwalk—until my right hand touched the angle of an iron ladder that dropped away into the engine-room depths.

With infinite care I worked my way off the catwalk and onto the rungs of the ladder below it. I started downward. It was a long, long climb. The deeper I went, the stronger the smell of oil and rust and stagnant water became. Finally I reached the floor of the engine room. I stayed there awhile, dragging air into my lungs.

When the pounding of my heart became less violent, it occurred to me that I hadn't heard anything from my pursuer for some time. I leaned against the bottom rungs of the ladder and listened for a few long minutes. There was no noise from above.

I felt along the floor of the engine room until I found an old rusty nail. I threw it, as hard as I could. It rang dully against something on the other side of the room.

The sound was followed instantly by the hard crack of a shot from the catwalk far above me. A bullet clanged off the bulkhead near where the nail had landed.

He had my Luger.

There was silence for about a minute. Then his heavy voice boomed from the catwalk: "Rome?"

I waited. More silence.

"You got nowhere to go," he called down. "You're stuck down there and you know it. Why not get smart and come on up and talk it over? There ain't anything between us we can't settle with some talk.''

He lied in his teeth.

Also, he didn't know much about ships if he thought I was trapped down there.

I began feeling my way across the engine room. Two stubbed toes, a bumped knee and a bruised shoulder later, I stumbled against what I was hunting for—the propeller shaft. I followed it toward the stern, one hand sliding along the shaft, the other hand held in front of me, head-high. When my hand was stopped by a solid bulkhead, I stooped, and felt my way forward into the shaft tunnel.

From there, all I had to do was keep moving straight ahead with the shaft, sliding one hand along the roof of the tunnel above me. Within a minute, my hand came upon the round emptiness of a manhole.

I got my feet and hands on the wet, slippery rungs of the ladder and began climbing up through the manhole, praying that the escape hatch at the top wouldn't be locked shut. I climbed till my head came against a solid barrier. The escape hatch. I shoved against it with my hand. It didn't budge. I pushed harder. The hatch gave a little. Not much, but enough to tell me it wasn't locked. The hinges were just frozen with rust.

Moving up another rung and bending my head down, I got my shoulders under the hatch and began forcing upward with my back and downward with my legs, straining to straighten up. The hatch gave way slowly, opening with a loud groaning from its rusted hinges. But the big blond with the limp was too far away to hear it, if he was still in the engine room.

I climbed out over the hatch coaming and squatted for a few moments in the dark passage above the manhole, getting my bearings. When I'd figured out my approximate position inside the ship, I went on to the next problem.

The other man had my gun. I had no weapon at all, and

I'd need one. A surprise attack is only as good as what's behind it. And he was both bigger and stronger than I.

Bending, I felt around the coaming till my fingers found the hatch securing screws. They turned out to be ordinary iron bolts, big and heavy. One was loose. I unscrewed it, wrapped my hand around its stem. That gave me a fistful of solid metal, with a hard protruding knob at one end. Enough to knock a man out with. Even an unusually large man.

I made my way through the black passage and up a flight of steps. Then along two more passageways and more steps. That brought me to the place where he'd attacked me with the fire ax. I found the doorway I'd dodged through and went down the steps there, my bare feet making not even a whisper of sound. The door to the engine room was open, and a fitful light came through it. I slid along the wall to the edge of the opening and looked down.

Below me was the flight of iron steps to the catwalk. He was on the catwalk, his back to me. I could see him clearly. He'd found a couple of mattresses and set them afire. One burned on the catwalk ten feet from him. He'd dropped the other to the floor of the engine room far below, where it was being consumed in its own blaze. My gun was in his hand. He was on one knee at the edge of the catwalk, looking down, trying to spot me by the light from the flaming mattresses.

I started down the steps behind him, one slow, careful step at a time. If I could reach the catwalk without him knowing it, and slug him with my fistful of heavy iron . . .

I didn't. Not finding me below, he raised his head and looked around, glowering. I was halfway down the steps to him when he saw me. He twisted around, straightening off his knee and bringing the Luger up at me.

I jumped. That was all I could do. I'd wanted to take him alive, but if one of us had to die it was not going to be me.

I came down on him feet-first. My heels rammed his broad

chest and knocked him backward. My momentum carried me with him. We went over the side of the catwalk together.

He went over head-first, his flailing arms whipping nothing but empty air. I went over feet-first, and my desperately clawing hands caught the edge of the catwalk. It stopped me, so suddenly my shoulders were almost torn from their sockets. My gripping fingers went numb with the shock and for an instant, as I heard the thud the big man made as he hit the bottom, I thought they weren't going to hold.

But they did hold. I dangled there under the catwalk, hanging full-length by my fingers, thinking of all that space under me. The thought brought life back into my arms. I hauled myself up laboriously and sprawled face-down on the catwalk, panting. Through its rusty iron slats I could see the other man lying on the engine-room floor. He didn't look so big, from that high up. He wasn't moving.

I finally climbed to my feet. My Luger lay on the catwalk where he'd dropped it. I picked it up and went along to the ladder and down to the engine-room floor.

He lay on his back, and I didn't need the Luger. Not against him. The fall had broken his neck.

Chapter 18

I WAS IN A SAVAGE MOOD WHEN I GOT ASHORE AND PHONED Art Santini. Three hours later I sat in his office at Homicide, gazing bleakly at the wall, and the mood hadn't lifted. Santini came in with a cardboard container of coffee in each hand. He didn't look too happy, either.

He lowered himself into the other chair and handed me one of the containers. "Same thing all over again," he growled. "No identification on blond boy. And nothing on Martin Roy that tells us who he was working for, or even where he's been living lately."

I swallowed a mouthful of hot coffee. "Dandy."

"Yeah," Santini said. "We'll send blond boy's fingerprints to Washington, of course. That didn't get us anywhere with his partner, but you never can tell."

I drank more coffee and went back to gazing at the wall.

After a time Santini said, "It's your own fault, you know. You could've let me in on it. I'd have gotten some of the boys and we could have gone to that freighter with you. We might have gotten one of them alive that way. Or even both of them."

"And then what? You didn't have anything you could arrest either one of them for."

"Might have been able to tie blond boy with Kovac's beating," Santini said.

"How? You said yourself the cab driver who saw him and

his partner leave the alley wouldn't be able to identify either of them in a line-up. Even if he did, it wouldn't hold up in court. He didn't see their faces.''

Santini sighed. ''There's still that business of Roy making that hole between his motel room and Carol Branco's, so he could shoot blackmail pictures.''

''That can't be proved, either. Not unless somebody finds the pictures he took, and I'd lay ten to one they've been destroyed by now. There's no way of proving that hole through the wall wasn't made by some previous tenant, in either room. No—they'd have just kept their mouths shut and any lawyer could have sprung them inside twenty-four hours. You wouldn't have gotten anything from either of them.''

Santini raised and lowered his shoulders. ''Well, we sure won't get anything out of them dead. Alive, there was always a chance.''

''Rub it in,'' I snarled. ''My masochistic streak needs the exercise.'' I finished my coffee and stood up. ''I'm going home to bed.''

I drove to Dinner Key and went aboard the *Straight Pass*, but I didn't go to sleep. The savage mood wouldn't let me. I kept thinking about Gil Hurley and Carol Branco and the missing .32 that had killed both of them. I could still put the pieces of the puzzle together several different ways. Without the vital missing piece, it remained guesswork.

Finally, I cast off from the pier and sailed north along the Florida coast toward Coffin City.

Two hours before dawn weariness took over. I moored the boat in a marina ten miles south of Coffin City, stretched out on my bunk, and slept. Four hours later the savage mood woke me and let me know it intended to keep me awake. I went for a swim, had breakfast in the marina, stuffed the small .22 inside the sleeve of my jacket, and continued north to Coffin City.

* * *

Serena Ferguson was coming out onto her porch when I arrived at her house. She looked very fresh in a tailored skirt and blouse the color of young oranges. I climbed the porch steps and she gave me her wide-eyed look and said, "You're back!"

"I am back," I agreed. "Are you on your way to work?"

She looked at me and said, "It can wait. You don't look so good. Black rings under your eyes."

"Too much frustration and not enough sleep. I could use some coffee."

Serena nodded. "There is some left in the pot. I'll get it."

She went inside, and I sat on a porch chair and looked at the trees. Big, well-fed, rich-neighborhood trees. They wouldn't have admitted even a nodding acquaintance with their poor relations on Mrs. Branco's street. Serena came out with the coffee, and we sat and drank and looked at each other.

"You're taking a frightful chance, coming back here now," she said.

"I know."

"Hollis Cobb was around looking for you. He's furious about what I put in the special edition—that you intended to prove Gil wasn't killed by the man who confessed to it, and that the confession was a police cover-up. Cobb said he'd make you sorry you said that."

I nodded. "That figures. It's the reason I came up by boat this time, instead of using the road. It'll take him longer to find out I'm around."

Serena frowned at me. "Where'd you leave your boat?"

"A place called Cottrell's Dock."

"Then Cobb will know you're back. Cottrell's on Tallant's payroll. Most of the men who cater to pleasure boats are. They steer tourists to Tallant's gambling places—and the other kind of places. That's another thing Mr. Kovac found out."

I leaned back and gave her a wry smile. "Thanks for letting me know, too late. Is there anything else I should know that you haven't gotten around to telling me?''

She thought about it, shook her head. "No. Not that I can think of.''

"Not even about Gil Hurley? Sure you didn't still have a crush on him?''

She looked at me gravely. "Quite sure. . . . I don't know why I like you. You're not very nice.''

"Frustration brings out the worst in me. Why did Hurley marry Willa?''

Serena looked down at her hands. "The usual reasons—I suppose.''

"There you go, feeding me more frustration.''

Serena looked up and smiled wanly. "All right—I think he married her for her money. Is that what you wanted me to say?''

"If it's true.''

"I'm fairly sure it is. Gil was always talking about getting into politics when he went with me. He knew how easily he could make people like him. He'd always been popular. He felt there was no limit to how far he could go—if he had enough financial backing. Willa gave him that. . . . Damn! I knew if I said it, it'd sound catty.''

"It just sounds like what it is," I told her. "The truth. And while you're in this truthful mood, what about that kiss between you and Hurley. He do much of that?''

"No. That was the only time—since he got married.''

I nodded and said, half to myself, "Yeah. He wouldn't want to start anything that could lead to emotional complications. His wife could always yank her money out from under him. And a scandal and divorce wouldn't help him to the governorship, either.''

I was thinking about that when Serena asked, "Why did you think that I still had a crush on Gil?''

My mind was on the other thing. "You seemed to respond pretty warmly in that clinch.''

She met my eyes steadily. "I'm normal. With healthy impulses. Or don't you think so?"

I grinned at her. "Healthiest girl I ever saw." I stood up. "Mind if I use your phone?"

"Go ahead. It's just inside, in the living room."

I went in and phoned Art Santini in Miami.

"Anything new?"

"Not much," Santini told me dispiritedly. "Just that the FBI had blond boy's prints on file. His name's Horace Craig and he's been a bad boy since he was twelve. Got a record from there to five years ago. Since then, nothing. But the FBI knows for a fact he became a syndicate enforcer. So it stands to reason his partner worked for the syndicate, too. For what it's worth, that's all we've got. And don't tell me it doesn't help any. Because I already know that."

I gazed at the wall, seeing things on it.

"You're wrong," I told Santini. "It does help."

I hung up the phone and took the puzzle apart and put it back together—the right way.

I had the missing piece now.

I went out to the porch and told Serena, "Thanks for the morning coffee and conversation. I'll be seeing you later."

She stood up and came over to me. "Where are you going?"

"To see Hollis Cobb."

It alarmed her. She gripped my arm and moved closer, the resilient swell of her breast touching me. "Do you have to?"

" 'Fraid so."

"You'll be careful?"

"Any specific suggestions?"

"Just be careful." She took my face between her hands and kissed me hard on the mouth. Then she pulled away and stepped back, her face flushed. "There! Does that convince you I didn't still have a crush on Gil?"

I smiled at her. "It convinces me you want to convince me, anyway."

She hit me with an indelicate two-word phrase that took on added shook value because it came from her. She turned on her heel and stalked off into the house. I left the porch and went to find acting Police Chief Hollis Cobb.

I didn't have to hunt far. He was waiting for me on the other side of the hedge, with his .45 in his hand. Deputy Luke LaFrance was there too, on the other side of me holding another .45 revolver. A city police car was parked behind my rented one.

Cobb jabbed his .45 at me and said tightly, "Open your jacket. With both hands."

I unbuttoned the jacket and held it wide open, turning my right arm so they wouldn't see the slight bulge inside the sleeve. Cobb removed the Luger from my belt holster and stuck it in his pocket. He gestured at the cop car.

"All right. Move."

We went to their car. LaFrance got in the back seat.

"In front," Cobb ordered me.

I slid into the front seat. Behind me, LaFrance rested his .45 on his knee, aimed at my back. Cobb stuck his gun in his holster and climbed behind the wheel next to me. He started the car and drove off.

"Long drive?" I asked tonelessly.

"For you," Cobb said nastily. "But Hugh Tallant wants to see you first."

"A few words before dying?"

"You can die right now," Cobb snapped, "if you don't sit quiet and not try anything."

"Be hard to explain," I pointed out carelessly.

"No it wouldn't. We'd just say you were shot while trying to resist arrest."

"Oh—am I under arrest? For what?"

"If it has to be explained, afterward," Cobb said, "it could be for murdering Gil Hurley."

"You've already got one patsy for that."

"He could change his mind. Say he was scared to tell the truth before."

"The truth being?"

"He was out there at the Coffin estate beach that night. But he didn't kill Hurley. He saw you do it."

I shook my head. "Won't hold water."

"Won't have to," Cobb informed me. "By then you'd be dead—for trying to escape from us after I charged you with the killing. I wouldn't have to prove a thing. So act nice and tame."

"So I can just vanish—buried out in the swamps somewhere? That way you wouldn't have to make any explanations at all."

Cobb didn't say anything to that.

I glanced behind me at LaFrance. "This is all right with you?"

LaFrance smiled that cherubic Santa Claus smile. "You've been a naughty boy, Rome. Shouldn't have said what you did in the *Clarion*. Made Hugh Tallant mad. And he warned you about that."

"Whatever happened to all that hot fervor to get the one who killed Hurley—the boy who used to go fishing with you when he was a kid?"

LaFrance frowned. "I meant that. I still mean it. If I ever find out who really did it . . . But that's got nothing to do with this. This is just politics. With you on the wrong side."

Cobb growled. "Stop running off at the mouth, Luke. Shut up—both of you."

We shut up. The car went west out of the city. Through the suburbs and trailer parks, across the highway, onto a narrow two-lane road leading deep into the Everglades. It grew hotter and muggier as we got farther from the sea. Dragonflies darted across the road. Low marshes stretched to the horizon on either side of us, with occasional palms and pines poking up out of the dense lower swamp vegetation. Every few miles or so along the road there'd be a farm where lawn grass was raised on ground made dry by dirt dikes and a deep drainage lake dug in the middle. Cobb turned the car off the road into one of these grass farms.

We pulled up in front of a solid white house with a windmill beside it, its blades turning lazily to the touch of a turgid breeze. Hugh Tallant appeared in the doorway. LaFrance climbed out of the car first, backing off a few steps and waiting for me with the .45 ready in his pudgy fist. I got out, and Cobb slid from behind the wheel and went around the front of the car to the other side of me. He didn't draw his gun again. One gun on me was enough.

Tallant came down the porch steps and walked slowly to us. Cobb put a heavy hand against my back and shoved me toward Tallant. We both stopped, a few feet apart, eyeing each other.

The eyes behind his steel-rimmed glasses were even colder than I remembered them. His tough, bony, muscular face was hard as stone.

"I gave you fair warning," he told me flatly. "I said there was a lot of mud out here in the swamps to lose you under if you got in my hair. But you didn't get me. You kept right on poking around and shooting your mouth off."

His eyes went the length of me, down, then up—taking their time. His mouth became thin.

"So now it's good-by, Rome."

Chapter 19

"JUST BECAUSE I SAID YOUR BEACH BUM DIDN'T KILL HURley?"

Tallant nodded. "Because you said you could prove it."

"I can."

"Too bad for you. We had a mess on our hands. We did a fast job of putting it in a bag and sewing it up tight. People were satisfied the bum shot Hurley; nobody was sore at us. Then you get ready to rip our bag open and scatter the mess around again. Only you're not going to."

"Don't you want to know who's responsible for Hurley's death?"

Tallant considered it. "Maybe. . . . But it won't change anything. We already rigged an answer to that. We can't go back on it—not before election."

"Somebody's been undermining your election plans all along," I told him. "Rigging it so the syndicate could move into Coffin City behind your back and boot you out. You've been fighting a long time to keep the syndicate out. The reform party's been working to get *you* out. But neither you nor the reform group was supposed to win this election. The syndicate was set to win it."

Tallant's lean figure stiffened. I had his full attention.

"It was a tricky plan," I said. "The idea behind it was for the syndicate to get a hold on Gil Hurley. A hold strong enough to force him to follow orders if he got elected Police

Chief. The orders would have been to make good his campaign promises by kicking all of your men off the police, closing down all your places, and putting you out of business. Then he was supposed to put in new cops who'd be on the syndicate payroll, and let the syndicate take over all your operations in Coffin City.''

I looked at the three of them—Tallant listening and thinking, Cobb scowling, LaFrance holding the gun on me.

"But first, they needed something they could use to pressure Hurley with. The simplest thing was to frame him with something he wouldn't want his wife to know about. Like getting pictures of him in bed with another woman. Hurley never gave much of a damn about cleaning up Coffin City. He only wanted to win the election as a springboard to becoming a state senator and eventually governor of the state. But he'd need the backing of his wife's money all the way to get there. He wouldn't want her to be shown proof that he wasn't faithful to her. She wouldn't like that. She'd most likely stop supporting him. She might even demand a divorce, creating a messy scandal that would wreck his political ambitions for good.''

"He's making this up," Cobb growled. "Just stalling. Hurley wouldn't have messed around with any woman at a time like this, with election coming up.''

"Not just any woman," I agreed. "That was the problem. But someone thought up a solution. Someone who knew Hurley was once going to marry a girl named Carol Branco, and that she ran out on him. Someone who also knew that Hurley was always crazy about her, never fell that hard again, and went on carrying a torch for her. The syndicate was informed of this, and two syndicate hoods went looking for Carol Branco.''

LaFrance heaved a bored sigh. "This is still just a story. Any of us could make up one just as good.''

"But I can prove this one," I said, and looked at Tallant. "Not proof that'd stand up in court, maybe. But proof enough for you. The two syndicate hoods I mentioned are the ones who beat up Lou Kovac. Because he was beginning to catch on about Carol Branco. They're both in the Dade County morgue now. You can check on what I said about them. One of 'em is named Horace Craig, and he was a known syndicate enforcer. It ought to be easy enough for somebody like you to check that, too.''

Tallant nodded and said very quietly, ''Go on.''

I took a slow breath. Their eyes and the gun were on me and my palms were feeling hot and heavy.

''One of the hoods found Carol Branco in Miami. The girl she was living with can tell you about that. He found out Carol Branco was perfect for what the syndicate wanted. She'd become a call girl and a dope addict. Not the kind of girl who could run to the cops for help. A girl who could be threatened with impunity, and who'd realize they'd carry out the threats if she didn't do what they wanted. So they were able to force her to come back here and help them frame Gil Hurley.''

''Still wouldn't work,'' Cobb said. ''Even if Hurley did carry a torch for her, he wouldn't wreck his political chances by getting involved with her and turning his rich wife against him.''

''Of course not. That's why she came back to Coffin City with that phony story about becoming a television star, and only being back for a month's vacation before returning to her career in New York. That way, she could seduce Hurley and he'd know he wasn't getting involved in anything that would last long enough to hurt him. He'd believe she was too intent on pursuing her new-found success to hang around and make things difficult. It would be just a pleasant, brief lovers' reunion. Then she'd be off to New York, and no one would ever know.

''Even so, Carol had to work hard to pull it off. Or maybe her reluctance to frame a man who'd loved her so much made it take longer. It probably didn't take long to get him to be with her in her mother's house during the days, when her mother was out working. I interrupted them there once. But apparently Hurley balked at going to her motel room at night. Because it took the photographer the syndicate planted in the next room almost three full weeks before he got the pictures he wanted. Hurley didn't know about that. They were going to spring it on him as a surprise, after he was elected.''

''How'd Kovac catch on to this?'' Tallant snapped. He was with me now, all the way, knowing what I said was true.

''I'm not sure. Maybe he saw Carol Branco with Hurley and got curious. Maybe he tailed her, spotted her with the syndicate's contact in Coffin City.''

''This contact got a name?'' Tallant demanded thickly.

I nodded. ''I'm getting to it. Somehow the syndicate contact found out Lou Kovac was getting wise. When Kovac went back to Miami to check on Carol Branco's background the two syndicate hoods were informed and told to put him out of action. They followed their orders. Kovac was put out of action. But then I showed up in Coffin City, ready to take over where Kovac left off.

''That really worried the syndicate contact. So I was shot at, and a stick of dynamite was wired to the ignition of my car.''

''By whom?'' Tallant grated. ''Stop playing it cute.''

''Figure it out for yourself,'' I told him. ''I'd only been in town a few hours when I was shot at. Who knew I was there, what I was up to, and where I was staying? I'd been to see Cobb. LaFrance had tailed me. You'd been informed of my presence. And Serena Ferguson, as editor of the *Clarion*, had read my ad and knew about me.''

I met Tallant's cold eyes, fighting against the squeezing tension inside me, trying to stay loose and ready to move.

''That makes four people that could have fired those shots at me,'' I told Tallant. ''Just four: You; Cobb; LaFrance; Serena Ferguson. . . . *You* certainly weren't working behind your own back to kick yourself out for the syndicate, so that lets you out.

"Serena Ferguson was too young at the time Carol Branco ran out on Hurley to know about it. And whoever thought up that plan had to have, beforehand, a complete personal acquaintance with what happened between Hurley and Carol over ten years back. So that lets her out.

"Cobb's an outlander. He's only been in Coffin City four years and wouldn't have known ancient history like a love affair between Hurley and Carol Branco—and how deep his passion for her went. So that lets Cobb out."

Luke LaFrance was still smiling. But he'd backed off two steps and raised his gun to cover all three of us by the time Cobb and Tallant turned to stare at him.

"Yeah," I said. "Jolly Luke LaFrance is the one who thought up the whole scheme, and worked it out with the syndicate. He's the one who sent those hoods to find Carol Branco and bring her back. And told them to smash Lou Kovac."

"Why?" Tallant demanded of him, puzzled. "Why would you, my own brother-in-law . . ."

LaFrance laughed. It wasn't a jolly laugh. His smile had become just a permanent exterior fixture with no meaning behind it. "Your brother-in-law! So what? You think I want to stay just a lousy deputy all my life? While my sister was alive, she could get you to give me a boost up now and then. Once she died, I was all washed up. I always figured I'd at least wind up Chief of Police, sooner or later. Then the Chief dies and what happens? You gave the job to *Cobb*. Well, brother-in-law, to hell with you."

"You're chuck full of loyalty," I told him. "Hurley used to go fishing with you when he was a kid. Remember?"

LaFrance shrugged an arm. Not the one holding the gun. "That's the way life goes. You got to grab your chances where they fall. But I didn't kill him."

"I know you didn't," I said. "But you rigged the rest of it. Everything I said."

Tallant was still trying to understand. "I never figured you to be that dumb, Luke. Going against me."

"Dumb? I'm not dumb. You'd have been out on your ear, Hugh. And who'd be running things in your place, once the syndicate took over? Me. That's what I was getting out of it. I was gonna run Coffin City for them."

"He's far from dumb," I told Tallant. "He's the one thought the whole thing up. A way for the syndicate to break you, and take over. And having rigged it so he could blackmail Hurley into obedience after the election, he even made sure it *would* be Hurley who got elected. Cobb's been playing around with an under-age girl in another county. LaFrance tipped the State cops about it. I suppose he intended to give them details later, so they'd catch Cobb redhanded with the girl just a few days before election. The scandal would have insured Hurley's winning."

"You're not so dumb yourself, Rome," LaFrance said. "Too bad it turned out this way. I liked your style from the start."

"The feeling," I told him thinly, "is not mutual. That was a good man your hoods beat to a pulp. You'll have to pay for that."

"Yeah?" He raised the .45 in his hand a bit. "You think so?"

Tallant and Cobb had begun drifting away from me—Cobb to my left, Tallant off to the right. That put me in the middle. But I wasn't the one about to make any sudden moves.

"Your mistake," I told LaFrance, "was in not getting Carol Branco out of Coffin City the second you had the pictures you wanted. You let her hang around to fill out the time she'd said she was vacationing here. Then when I began asking questions about her, too many people began wondering what she was really up to. One of them put a couple things together—with the result that Gil Hurley was killed. After that you had to send your hoods to find Carol Branco, if they could, and kill her. And stop me from finding her first. You knew if I or the cops got her, and squeezed her about Hurley, she'd spill everything. . . .''

I stopped talking and dived for the ground, shaking the little .22 out of my sleeve as I landed. Because at that moment Tallant and Cobb had jumped farther away to either side of me, going for their guns.

Cobb got his out first. But he didn't get time to use it before LaFrance's .45 boomed. The heavy slug smashed through Cobb's face. He dropped like a huge puppet with its strings cut, dying before he hit the ground.

By then I had the .22 automatic up, and was taking careful aim. LaFrance twisted his fat figure toward me, bringing the .45 around. I squeezed the trigger. The .22 made a sharp little noise, like a firecracker. The bullet went through his right wrist, spilling the gun from his hand.

LaFrance gasped and seized his torn wrist with his good hand.

He was unarmed and helpless when Hugh Tallant shot him in the stomach.

LaFrance fell back against the car and pressed both arms hard against his middle, his mouth straining wide with agony. I jerked around and aimed the .22 at Tallant's face a split-second before he could train his gun on me. He froze, holding the gun; studying me and thinking it over. I got up on one knee, still holding my aim on him.

"That's not much of a gun," he said thoughtfully. "One shot won't do me that much damage. I can kill you before you get in another shot."

"I'm aiming at your left eye," I told him. "Even a twenty-two'll go in through there. And keep going, through your brain. There won't be anything to stop it until it hits the back of your skull."

I stood up. "Now let your gun fall."

He continued to watch me and think about it, not moving.

I took a step toward him, the .22 staying on his eye.

"What the hell," he said, casually, and let go of the gun. "Why should I take the chance? My lawyer can get me off. I shot him in self-defense."

I picked up his gun—careful not to smudge his finger-prints—and backed away from him. "Not on my testimony. He was unarmed when you fired."

Tallant shrugged. "I'll still get away with it, once I'm in court."

"Maybe," I said. "Maybe not. One thing is sure. You won't be winning any elections around here for some years to come."

LaFrance had sagged to the ground and was doubled up, whimpering with pain. "Oh, Christ, it hurts. . . . Get me a doctor. . . . Please . . . I need a doctor . . ."

"Lou Kovac needed a lot of doctors," I told him coldly. "He still does."

LaFrance sobbed and pressed his blood-soaked hands harder against his stomach wound. I kicked his gun and Cobb's into a drainage ditch, put the .22 in my pocket and got my Luger from Cobb's pocket. Then I marched Tallant inside the house and called Lieutenant Waine. I told him where we were, outside the limits of Coffin City, and that he could come pick up Hugh Tallant for killing one of his own deputies. As an afterthought, I told him to bring a doctor.

LaFrance wasn't dead yet, when we went back outside. But he was on his way. By the time the doctor arrived, he was no longer needed.

Chapter 20

IT WAS LATE AFTERNOON WHEN I ARRIVED AT MRS. BRAN-
co's house. She wasn't in, so I sat in the porch rocker and
waited. I was in no hurry to see her. It's never pleasant to
spend time with someone grieving over the death of an only
child. But I felt I should.

Time passed slowly, lazily. Now that it was all over I was
experiencing the aftermath of supreme tension held too long.
Weariness gradually flowed through my veins. I felt like a
vessel that had been battered and whirled around by a long
storm, and suddenly left in a quiet backwater, still intact,
after the storm had passed.

Mrs. Branco drove up in front of her house in an old Chevy.
I stood up as she came toward her porch. She had aged a
decade since I had last seen her. Her lined face looked empty,
drained of the last strong emotions life would ever hold for
her. She moved with the heaviness of deep fatigue.

Climbing onto the porch, she stared at me blankly for a
moment before recognizing me. "The reporter . . ." she
said emptily. "You want to do a story in your newspaper on
my daughter's death?"

"No," I told her. "I'd like to offer my sympathy, Mrs.
Branco. I know what a shock it must have been for you.
Other people's sympathy doesn't help much at a time like
this. But for what it's worth, you have mine."

"Thank you," she said mechanically, in a tired voice. "I . . . Won't you come in?"

I nodded, uncomfortably. She unlocked the door and we entered the room where Hurley and Carol Branco, frightened of being found out, had blinded me with a blanket and fled, leaving me unconscious on the floor. Nothing in it had changed. The silver-framed portrait photo was still there.

"Would you like some coffee?" Mrs. Branco asked.

"No. Don't bother."

"No bother. I need some for myself. I've just come from attending to the . . . funeral arrangements."

She moved off slowly into the kitchen. I sat on the edge of the studio couch. Carol Branco's eyes, in the picture, seemed to watch me. I wanted to smoke, but didn't.

Mrs. Branco came back with coffee on a tray. She put the tray on a little table in front of the studio couch, sat across from me and poured coffee into our cups. She picked up her cup and sipped. I didn't touch mine.

She put her cup down and looked at the portrait of her daughter for what seemed a long time. "Did you ever get to write anything in your paper about her?"

I took a slow breath. "I'm not actually a reporter, Mrs. Branco. I'm a private detective."

She looked at me, puzzlement making a deep crease between her eyes. "I don't understand. . . . I don't understand any of it—what's happened . . . why my daughter is dead. Do you know?"

I nodded, and began telling her the background to her tragedy, most of the things I'd told Tallant. She listened as I talked, trying to grasp what I was saying.

Finally she shook her head. "That's not my daughter you're talking about," she said weakly, not sure what she believed any longer. "My daughter wouldn't have been a . . . She was an actress. She was going to be a TV star."

"You must know by now that isn't true," I told her gently. "Don't you know why your daughter killed herself?"

She stared at me like a small sparrow suddenly confronted by a very large snake. She didn't say anything.

"You shouldn't have dressed her," I said. "You put somebody else's clothes on her. What did you do with the gun?"

Her eyes became blank. Her continued silence took on a frozen quality.

"It had to be that way," I said quietly. "When I told Gil Hurley about the hole in the wall between your daughter's motel room and the next room, and what it probably meant, it wasn't hard for him to put two and two together. He suddenly realized what had been done to him. Someone had taken pictures of him together with your daughter, pictures that could be used to blackmail him later. The thought must have terrified him. He had to know the truth. He waited till everyone else had gone to sleep that night, and then he phoned your daughter at her motel. She got a call at one in the morning and drove away from her motel. One hour later, Gil Hurley was killed."

It was impossible to go on sitting there with Mrs. Branco watching me the way she was. I got up and paced to the windows, stared through them, seeing nothing by my image of how it must have happened.

"Hurley probably told her nothing over the phone, except that he had to see her, and where to meet him. She met him at the boat dock on the Coffin estate, and there he told her what I'd found out and demanded an explanation. I don't imagine it was hard for him to get the truth out of her. She'd been forced into framing him; she must have hated what she was being made to do to a man who'd loved her—and perhaps still did. When he knew the truth, it must have overwhelmed him with a violent mixture of fear and rage. His whole future might go down the drain because your daughter had used his passion for her to pull him into a coldly planned trap.

"The shock of knowing what a fool he'd been, that he'd been played for a sucker, that he might be about to lose everything he'd wanted or spend the rest of his life under a blackmailer's thumb—caused him to completely lose control of himself. He attacked her in a blind, vengeful fury. He struck her with his fist. The bruise was on his knuckles and there was a bruise on her face where he hit her. He started to strangle her—judging by the marks on her throat. She scratched his face, but he wouldn't stop—perhaps couldn't stop himself.

"She felt he was going to kill her, and maybe he would have. She got the gun from his pocket while he was strangling her, and she shot him with it. I don't think it was a conscious act, even if it was justifiable as self-defense. It was the blind instinct of self-preservation, taking control over her actions when she was too dazed to know what she was doing. But she shot him. And he died."

I turned and looked at Mrs. Branco's bent figure. Her face was taut and expressionless now. But she was listening, and thinking.

"I knew for certain," I said, "that she had killed Hurley, once I learned they'd both been killed by the same gun—his gun. None of the people who might have had a reason to kill Hurley would have had any way to find your daughter at that beach cabin she'd hidden herself in. The men who might have found her there—hoodlums working for the syndicate—would have had no reason to kill Hurley. They wanted him to become Coffin City's Chief of Police. And both your daughter and Hurley were killed by the same person—twenty-four hours apart—with the gun taken from Hurley's pocket.

"She probably didn't realize she still had the gun in her hand as she ran away after seeing that Hurley was dead. Not till she got in her car. Then she probably dropped it on the seat beside her, not thinking in her panic, and drove away.

"She'd killed a man, and she thought the police would be coming after her. She knew that killers working for Luke LaFrance and the syndicate would be after her. With Hurley dead, they couldn't take the chance of her telling about the blackmail scheme they'd rigged to oust Tallant. She went to that beach cabin. Once she was there, she had the whole day in which to think—and come to the conclusion that there was nothing she could do, nowhere she could go. She must have been horribly tired before the day was done. Emotional exhaustion, and not having had any sleep at all the night before. And on top of that, an increasingly demanding craving for heroin. She was deeply addicted, and she had none with her. Her one attempt to get someone to bring her some failed. She was afraid to go to her usual sources, because the syndicate's killers might be there waiting for her.

"She took off her clothes and lay down and tried to sleep. But she couldn't. Her nerves and the hunger for dope and her thoughts wouldn't let her. She must have thought a long time about the mess she'd made of her life. Ending with double-crossing a fairly decent man who'd loved her, and killing him. And knowing that professional killers were after her must have made her feel like a hunted animal. She could have gone to the police, pleaded self-defense and demanded protection. But she wouldn't do that, knowing they'd take her off drugs and that she wouldn't be able to stand it. Also, police protection goes just so far and lasts just so long. She knew the syndicate had a long memory and a longer arm.

"A woman who lived with your daughter for a time told me she was subject to black, suicidal moods. Under the circumstances, it's understandable that she fell prey to the worst one of her life. She could see no future for herself. Despair, and self-hatred, and disgust with life in general would have dictated her final move. She got Hurley's gun, put it to her temple, and killed herself with it.

"But first, she must have phoned *you*."

For perhaps a minute, Mrs. Branco said nothing. Then she straightened herself in the chair and looked at me. There was nothing in her face but weary relief.

"Yes," she said, "Carol called me."

I walked back to the studio couch and sat down, meeting her eyes and waiting.

"I'm glad to tell somebody," she said, in a small, taut voice. "It hurt so much, holding it in. How did you know?"

"The contact powder burns on her temple—and what I told you about her and Hurley being killed with the same gun—told me she'd probably killed herself. If so, where was the gun? And why was she wearing another woman's clothes? She wouldn't have put on someone else's things to kill herself in. Why would she? Why would anyone put them on her, after she was dead? Except you. You didn't know they weren't her clothes in the closet there. And you didn't want the police to find her undressed."

"No," Mrs. Branco said softly. "It wouldn't have been nice."

"And no one else would have had a reason to take away the gun, so it wouldn't look like a suicide. *You* could have had reasons, though I'm not sure which ones you acted on."

I waited, watching her think about it. Finally she looked at her daughter's portrait and said in a dead-flat voice, "She called me on the phone that night. She sounded . . . I never heard her like that before . . . She said that some terrible people had forced her to do something she didn't want to do, and now she was in bad trouble. It was so bad there was no way out of it for her—except to kill herself. . . . She didn't want to lie where she was with nobody knowing—maybe dead for weeks before anyone came and found her. She told me where she was, so I'd know. . . ."

Mrs. Branco looked down at her hands, turned them over and looked at their worn palms. "I tried to talk her out of it . . . I *begged* her not to—to wait till I got there. But I don't think she heard me. She sounded . . . like she wasn't in her right mind. I still hoped. I hurried and got dressed and rushed out to my car and drove down there. But I was too late. She was already dead."

"So you got a skirt and sweater from the closet and put them on her."

Mrs. Branco nodded. "I wanted her to look decent."

"And you took the gun out of her hand. What did you do with it?"

"I threw it in the ocean. Then I came home. I was going to wait a while, then call the State Police. I would have told them to go to that cabin, that they'd find someone there who'd been killed. I'd have hung up without telling them who I was."

"So the police would go there, find her dead and no weapon, and assume she'd been murdered. Why did you want them to think that, Mrs. Branco?"

She rubbed her stiff-held hands together, slowly, hunting for the words to tell me what words couldn't fully explain.

"Everybody here thought Carol was a successful actress," she said haltingly. "I wanted them to go on thinking of her that way. If she'd committed suicide, people would wonder why. They'd figure nobody who was about to become a big star would suddenly kill herself for no reason."

"That was your only reason?" I asked gently, knowing it wasn't. She hadn't been thinking clearly at the time. She would have wanted contradictory things.

"No . . . Carol had said that some terrible people were responsible for getting her into trouble, making her want to kill herself. I thought—if I made it look like murder—the police might find those terrible people and punish them. I wanted them punished for what they did to my Carol."

I drew a deep breath and let it out slow. "You succeeded," I told her. "Those terrible people were found. They've been punished—as much as you could ever have wanted them to be."

Vindictiveness blazed briefly in her eyes. Her mouth drew thin and hard. "That's good . . . I'm glad."

The flare of anger left her, to be replaced by wariness. "You couldn't make me tell the police what I've told you, you know. I could deny it. And then you could never prove my daughter committed suicide. . . . Could you?"

"I could. If I told the police all I know, they'd make chemical tests of her hands. They'd find traces of nitrate, to prove that she'd fired a gun. They'd dive and find the gun.''

Mrs. Branco's eyes narrowed at me. ''Are you going to tell them?''

I shook my head. ''No, Mrs. Branco. I can't think of any reason why I should.''

She continued to study me, until she was satisfied that I was telling her the truth. Then she picked up her cup, and leaned back and looked at my cup.

''You're not drinking your coffee,'' she said. ''It'll go cold.''

I took my cup and sipped. It was still warm. We sat there drinking coffee together and looking at the silver-framed picture of her daughter.

About the Author

Marvin H. Albert was born in Philadelphia and has lived in New York, Los Angeles, London, Rome, and Paris. He currently lives on the Riviera with his wife, the French artist Xenia Klar. He has two children, Jan and David.

He has been a Merchant Marine Officer, actor and theatrical road manager, newspaperman, magazine editor, and Hollywood script writer, in addition to being the author of numerous books of fiction and nonfiction.

Several of his novels have been Literary Guild choices. He has been honored with a Special Award by the Mystery Writers of America. Nine of his novels have been made into motion pictures.

TAF-106